## DATE DUE

| | |
|---|---|
| AUG 2 1 1995 | MAR 1 1 2005 |
| SEP 2 9 1995 | AUG 1 0 2007 |
| NOV 1 6 1995 | AUG 0 6 2008 |
| MAY 2 3 1996 | SEP 2 4 2009 |
| JUL 1 1 1996 | |
| AUG 0 8 1996 | |
| MAY 1 5 1997 | |
| MAY 2 2 1997 | |
| JUN 2 0 1997 | |
| NOV 0 6 1997 | |
| JUL 3 0 1998 | |
| JUL 3 0 1999 | |
| MAY 2 5 2000 | |
| SEP 0 6 2001 | |
| AUG 2 6 2003 | |
| SEP 2 0 2003 | |
| JUL 0 2 2004 | |

Look for:

*Wordsworth and the . . .*

*Cold Cut Catastrophe*
*Kibble Kidnapping**
*Roast Beef Romance**
*Mail-Order Meatloaf Mess**

From HarperPaperbacks

* coming soon

# Wordsworth and the Cold Cut Catastrophe

## by Todd Strasser

HarperPaperbacks
*A Division of HarperCollinsPublishers*

HarperPaperbacks   *A Division of* HarperCollins*Publishers*
                    10 East 53rd Street, New York, N.Y. 10022

Cover and interior illustrations by Leif Peng
Cover and interior art ©1995 Creative Media Applications, Inc.

First HarperPaperbacks printing: April 1995

Printed in the United States of America

HarperPaperbacks and colophon are trademarks of
HarperCollins*Publishers*

❖ 10 9 8 7 6 5 4 3 2 1

*To Nancy Baron,*
*dedicated teacher and wonderful human being*

# One

**Did I ever tell you about the time** the Chandlers found out they had no money? Oh, of course not. Why, you don't even know who I am. My name's Wordsworth. Maxwell Short Wordsworth the Sixth, to be exact. I live with the Chandlers. They are not as fancy as the families my parents and grandparents belonged to. But the Chandlers ask little of me. I am not asked to hunt, or fetch sticks, or do silly tricks for dog biscuits. And they feed me quite well.

All in all, it's not a bad life.

For a basset hound.

Yes, that is what I am. One of those strong handsome canines with long ears and sturdy legs. Basset hounds have served kings and queens. We have proved ourselves brave and loyal in wars. We are powerful and quick. And surely the smartest four-footed creatures on the planet.

Actually, I think we're smarter than most two-footed creatures as well. Which brings me back to my story about the Chandlers.

It all started on a sunny afternoon in late June. A light breeze made the leaves on the trees flutter. Small white clouds floated in the blue sky above. I was lying on the warm flagstones on the Chandlers' patio, soaking in the sunlight. Mrs. Chandler was sitting in the backyard with her oil paints and her easel.

Mrs. Chandler's first name is Flora. She was painting a picture of a large dandelion. She was wearing a white sun hat with a wide brim. Her long blond hair fell down her back. She was humming to herself, as usual.

Roy, the Chandlers' fourteen-year-old son, was also in the backyard. He was pushing a hand lawn mower. The Chandlers own a power mower, but Roy insists on using the hand machine. He thinks this will help him grow big muscles. Why he wants big muscles is beyond me.

And then there was Dee Dee Chandler, aged ten. She is my personal favorite. Dee Dee pays more attention to me than all the other Chandlers combined. She feeds and walks me, clips my nails, and brushes me. She makes sure I am taken along on family trips. And she always insists, bless her heart, that I never be put in a kennel.

# Wordsworth and the Cold Cut Catastrophe

At that moment Dee Dee was putting together an awful-looking thing called a dog run. It was a wire strung between the fence and a tree in the backyard. If I have one complaint about Dee Dee, it's that she cares *too* much about me. I wish that she wouldn't listen to that silly veterinarian Dr. Hopka, who always tells her I'm too heavy, and not getting enough exercise.

"I'm finished, Wordsworth." Dee Dee came toward me. She is a cute girl with blond hair. "Now we can leave you in the backyard when we're not around."

The backyard has a fence, but it's old and has fallen down in a few places. Dee Dee has this odd idea that if she leaves me alone I might run away.

"Now you can run up and down outside all day long," she said.

Run? Me? She *had* to be kidding.

# Two

**I rolled over on my back, hoping Dee**
Dee would give my tummy a good scratch and forget about this running nonsense. But instead she clipped a leash to my collar. The other end of the leash was attached to the wire.

"Come on, try it," she said.

Fat chance. I rolled back onto my stomach, yawned, and closed my eyes. I wanted to finish my nap.

"Please, Wordsworth," Dee Dee begged. She got down on her hands and knees and pressed her face close to mine. "Dr. Hopka says you don't get enough exercise."

Dr. Hopka didn't know his nose from his elbow. I happened to be in excellent physical shape.

"Darling?" a voice said.

Dee Dee and I looked up. Dee Dee's father, Leyland

Chandler, had come into the backyard. Leyland is a thin man with long white hair. He was wearing a heavy brown apron with pockets for tools, and on his head was a pair of clear goggles. Leyland spends most of his time in his workshop in the basement. We were surprised to see him out in the sun.

"Yes, dear?" Flora looked up from her dandelion painting.

Leyland shielded his eyes with his hand. He isn't used to bright sunlight. "The bank just called. They say all our checks are bouncing."

"That's odd." Flora's smooth forehead wrinkled. She pressed the dry end of a paintbrush against her lips.

Dee Dee started to scratch my head. "Are they made of rubber?" she asked.

"No, dear," her mother said. "When checks bounce it means there isn't enough money in our checking account."

"Actually, the man at the bank says we have no money at all," Leyland said.

"Did he say what happened to it?" Dee Dee asked.

"He said we spent it," her father replied.

"All of it?" Flora looked surprised.

"Well, whatever we had," said Leyland.

You may be wondering how a family can run out of money. Let me explain that the Chandlers are different from the other families in the neighborhood.

# Wordsworth and the Cold Cut Catastrophe

In most other families, the father, or the mother, or both, go to work. Sometimes when I get up early in the morning I see them walking to the train station. They wear suits or dark dresses, and carry newspapers and briefcases.

The Chandlers never get up before ten in the morning. Almost every day, Leyland goes down to the basement and works on "inventions." Flora paints in the backyard. But the Chandlers do have something called an "inheritance." And that is supposed to give them money.

"Can't we get more?" Flora asked. She was talking about money.

"Yes, but not for several months," Leyland said. "Apparently there's been some kind of accounting error."

"What will we do?" Flora asked.

Leyland ran his fingers through his long white hair. "I think we should talk about it at dinner." Then he turned and went back into the house.

Flora went back to her painting. Dee Dee scratched behind my ear—one of my favorite spots. A few seconds later Roy pushed the lawn mower over the dandelion his mother was painting, cutting it in two.

"Roy, dear?" Flora looked up from the easel.

"Yeah, Mom?"

"I'm afraid you've just decapitated my dandelion."

Roy looked down and saw the dandelion shreds lying among the grass clippings. "Oh, sorry, Mom."

"It's all right, dear," Flora said. "I was getting tired of painting it anyway." She started to screw the little black caps back on her tubes of paint.

"Mom?" Dee Dee said.

"Yes, dear?"

"What does it mean if we don't have any money?"

Flora thought for a moment. "Well, it means we won't be able to buy things."

"Like what?"

"Like food, and clothes, and paint."

"What about food for Wordsworth?" Dee Dee was always thinking of me, bless her heart.

"I'm afraid we won't have money for him either," Flora said.

That was when I realized how serious the situation was.

# Three

**That night the Chandlers sat down** for dinner. Dinner at the Chandlers' house is unlike the dinners other families eat. At other homes, the mother, or father, or the cook, makes a large meal that the family shares. At the Chandlers', dinner means that each member of the family makes whatever he or she feels like eating.

Flora made a salad for herself. Leyland had a large bowl of cold soup with sour cream. Roy made himself two triple-decker peanut-butter-and-jelly sandwiches. Dee Dee made me a lamb chop and herself a bowl of cornflakes. Janine brought a meatball sub from the sub shop in town.

I forgot to mention Janine. She is Dee Dee's and Roy's older sister. Like her mother, she has long blond hair, and is quite pretty. She is also very popular, judging from the number of phone calls she gets each day. Most of the time Janine doesn't answer the phone because she's not home. She is usually off somewhere playing one sport or another.

At dinner that night, Janine sat with her chin in her hand and hardly touched her sub. I was lying on the floor nearby, wondering how I could get my paws on that delicious-looking sandwhich.

"How was your day?" Leyland asked.

"I beat Alexandra Chapin at tennis this morning," Janine said. "Then this afternoon I played volleyball. After dinner I'm playing softball."

Janine was wearing a blue baseball hat, a white softball shirt, gray stretch pants, and black cleats.

"Sounds like you had a very exciting day," her father said.

Janine nodded. She looked glum.

"Is something wrong, dear?" Flora asked.

"Alexandra said you and Dad were out to lunch," Janine said.

Flora and Leyland looked at each other and scowled.

"But that's not true," Flora said. "We had lunch at home today."

"No, Mom," Roy said. "Out to lunch means you're weird."

"That's just sour grapes," Leyland said. "After all, didn't you say you beat her at tennis?"

Janine sighed and picked at her sub. To my great disappointment, it looked like she was going to eat it after all.

Leyland turned to Roy. "And how was your day?"

Roy shrugged. "I cut the grass and watched TV."

"Was anything good on?" Leyland asked.

"Naw, just the same old game shows and soap operas," Roy said.

I should add that Roy doesn't just watch the TV. He watches it and lifts weights at the same time. He's only been doing this for a few months. Every night before he goes to bed, he stands in front of the mirror and tries to make his muscles bulge. So far, no bulge.

"And you?" Leyland asked Dee Dee.

"Kristen and I rode our bikes in the park and then we played with her toy horses," Dee Dee said.

"Sounds like everyone had a very nice day," Flora said.

"Except," Leyland reminded her.

Flora looked puzzled for a moment, then remembered. "Oh, yes, the money."

"What about it?" Janine asked.

"I'm afraid I have some rather troubling news," Leyland said. "We've run out of it and probably won't get any more for several months."

"Wow, what are we going to do?" Roy asked.

Leyland glanced at Flora. "Well, uh, to be honest, we're not sure. I was hoping you children might have some suggestions."

Just then the phone rang. Everyone looked at Janine, since almost every phone call was some boy looking for her.

"Can't someone else answer it?" Janine asked.

"What's the point?" Roy said.

"Maybe if we just let it ring, it will stop," Janine said.

But the phone continued to ring, and the Chandlers continued to stare at it.

"I have a feeling it's not going to stop," Flora said.

"Janine's probably got a new boyfriend," said Roy.

"I do not," Janine said. To prove it, she got up and answered the phone.

"Hello? Oh, just a minute." Janine put her hand over the receiver. "It's for you," she said to Leyland.

"Who is it?" Leyland frowned. He wasn't used to getting phone calls.

"Burt Pulsky."

"Who?"

"From the Payup Collection Company," Janine said, and handed her father the phone.

"Collection company?" Leyland looked puzzled as he took the phone. "But I don't collect anything. . . . Hello?"

A man with a gruff voice began to speak. His voice was so loud that the whole family could hear it. The man was telling Leyland that he owed money.

"Yes, I'm aware of that," Leyland replied. "The problem is that we've run out."

The man said he didn't care. If the bills weren't paid he was going to take Leyland to court. By the time Leyland got off the phone, he looked pale and shaken.

# Four

**"Is it serious?" Flora asked as Leyland** settled down at the table again.

"I'm afraid so," Leyland replied.

"You should have told him to get lost, Dad," Roy said.

"Roy, darling," Flora gently scolded him. "We don't say that to people."

"Well, he wasn't being very nice to Dad," Roy replied.

"Two wrongs don't make a right, dear," Flora said.

"What are we going to do?" Dee Dee asked.

"We'll pay our bills as soon as we get some money," Leyland said.

"He didn't sound like he was willing to wait," Janine said.

"Besides, how are we going to eat for the next few months?" Roy asked.

Leyland and Flora gazed across the table at each other.

"I suppose I could go down to the workroom and see if there are any inventions I could sell," Leyland said.

The rest of the family gave each other doubtful looks. Every once in a while Leyland puts on his blue suit, packs up one of his "inventions," and goes somewhere to try to sell it. But he always returns a day or two later, still carrying the invention. Then he sits around in a bathrobe and mopes for a week before going back down to his workroom and starting on something new.

The same is true of Flora. Every spring and fall she packs a bunch of her paintings in the car and goes to an art show where she tries to sell them. Four or five days later she returns with almost all of them. Then she paints them all white, lets them dry, and paints over them.

"I hate to say this, Dad," said Janine, "but no one's ever bought one of your inventions."

"Maybe I could sell some paintings," Flora said.

No one seemed to think that would work either.

"I know!" Roy said. "Let's have a carnival! We could have rides and sell cotton candy and stuff. We'll invite all the kids in the neighborhood."

"A carnival?" Leyland frowned.

"Yeah, and we could have a kissing booth," Roy continued. "Janine could sit in the booth and boys would pay to kiss her. We'd make a ton of money."

"Sounds awfully unhygienic." Flora made a face.

"No way," said Janine.

"It beats starving," Roy said.

"Why don't we put *you* in the kissing booth," Janine said.

"Then we won't make a penny," said Dee Dee.

"Thanks, Dee Dee." Roy sniffed.

"Children, please don't hurt each other's feelings," Flora said. Then she turned to her husband. "Leyland, this situation is clearly upsetting the children. We must think of something."

# Five

**Dinner ended and the family still had** no firm idea about how to make money. Finally Leyland said he would go to the bank the next day and ask about a loan.

After dinner Janine put her half-eaten sub on the kitchen counter and went off to play softball with her friends. Roy went upstairs to lift weights and watch more television. Leyland and Flora went into the den, where they usually spent their evenings reading books and playing cards.

I closed my eyes and pretended to snooze. But as soon as Dee Dee left the kitchen, I got up and hurried over to the counter. I got up on my hind legs and pressed my front paws against the dishwasher. I got my nose over the counter. Janine's sub was just inches away!

"What are you doing, Wordsworth?" Dee Dee asked, coming back into the kitchen with my leash.

I quickly got down.

"You were trying to get Janine's sub," Dee Dee said. "How can you still be hungry? You just ate dinner."

I could *always* still be hungry.

"Janine's going to be starved when she gets home," Dee Dee said. "We have to save this for her."

Dee Dee put the sub in the refrigerator, then turned to me.

"Come on, Wordsworth, let's go for a walk."

I gave her the saddest look possible.

"Don't look at me like that," Dee Dee said as she clipped the leash to my collar. "You know what Dr. Hopka said. You have to get some exercise and lose weight."

I reminded myself to give Dr. Hopka a good hard nip the next time I saw him.

We went out the front of the house and down the steps. Usually I liked rubbing my tummy on the steps, but the front steps are wooden. Sometimes you can get a splinter.

The Chandlers live in an area called Soundview Manor. The houses here are all large and old. They're surrounded by big trees and lush gardens. Soundview Manor is close to Bell Island Sound. On a sunny summer day you will often see more sailboats on the Sound than you can count. All in all, it is a very pleasant place for a dog to live.

Except for our neighbors.

The house next door belongs to Charles Pickney,

the mayor of Soundview Manor. His wife, Claire, heads the town beautification committee. They have a son named Adam.

"Whoa, dudes, check this out!" a voice said as Dee Dee and I passed the Pickney house. Adam was sitting on the front steps with some of his friends, smoking cigarettes. They were wearing black T-shirts and jeans, and some of them had tattoos and earrings. Adam wore a black bandanna on his head. He had a small gold hoop in his nose.

"Looks like Dee Dee is taking Heavy Sausage for a walk," Adam said. His friends snickered.

"Hey, Dee Dee, is that cute-looking sister of yours around?" Adam called.

"Get lost, Adam," Dee Dee said.

"How can I get lost?" Adam asked. "I'm sitting in front of my own house."

"That never stopped you before," Dee Dee said.

Adam's friends laughed. His face turned red. He muttered something angrily and came down the walk toward us. His friends got up and followed.

"Why don't you get yourself a real dog?" Adam sneered. "Instead of this overfed waddling meat loaf?"

I would have taken a good-size bite out of his leg, but I knew it would only get the Chandlers into trouble.

"Wordsworth happens to be the best dog in the world," Dee Dee said, petting me lovingly on the head. "And he's an exceptional guard dog."

"Whoa, dudes," Adam said with a laugh. "Heavy Sausage isn't just a regular guard dog. He's an *exceptional* guard dog! The only thing I don't understand is, what do *you* need a guard dog for?"

He turned to his friends and pointed at the Chandlers' house. "Who'd want to break into that wreck?"

I'm afraid he had a good point. The Chandlers' house was in terrible condition. The white paint was peeling off the walls in big flakes. The shutters hung at strange angles to the windows. The porch steps were falling down and the lawn was a wasteland of weeds and brown spots.

"What an eyesore," said Joseph, a long-haired friend of Adam's.

"That house should be condemned," said another kid I didn't know.

"Or torched," added the third.

"My old man says our house would be worth twice as much if it wasn't next to that piece of junk," Adam said.

There was probably some truth to that. The Pickneys' house is a large stately white Colonial with dark blue trim. The lawn is a perfect carpet of green grass and the gardens are filled with beautiful flowers.

"Well, I'd rather be me living in my house than be you living in the Taj Mahal," Dee Dee shot back.

Once again Adam's friends laughed.

Adam's face turned red. He bent down so that he was looking right into Dee Dee's eyes. "You think you're pretty smart for a little kid, don't you? Well, I'd watch your mouth if I were you. Or someday you're gonna wake up and Heavy Sausage here is gonna be squashed flatter than a pancake."

# Six

**I wasn't sorry to leave Adam and his** friends. I have often suspected that Adam put fire-crackers in cats' ears and fed dogs hamburger meat mixed with Drāno. Dee Dee and I continued our walk down Magnolia Street. We passed the stately houses with their tall iron fences and thick green hedges.

Dee Dee often talked to me when we went out for a walk. I don't think she expected me to answer, so I never did. Instead I sniffed around, hoping to pick up a tasty morsel someone had left on the street.

"I'm really worried about the money, Wordsworth," she said. "Mom and Dad mean well, but I don't think they have a clue about what to do. They've never had money problems before."

It was a warm June evening and we soon ran into my friends, who were also out for walks with their owners.

# Wordsworth and the Cold Cut Catastrophe

There was Cody, the yellow Lab who lived across the street. She was out of breath because she'd been chasing squirrels in the park. And there was Madison, the dark brown dog who'd just come back from playing with Cookie, the black Collie down the block. Then I ran into Fluffy, the golden retriever from around the corner.

"Great news!" she barked eagerly.

"What?" I asked, slowing down.

Dee Dee and Fluffy's owner were going in different directions. They started to tug on our leashes.

"Come on, Wordsworth," Dee Dee grunted, pulling me away. I dug my nails into the pavement. Fluffy's owner was pulling her away, too.

"Let's get tangled," Fluffy suggested.

"Good idea," I said.

We raced around each other in a tight circle, getting our leashes tangled.

"Stop it, Fluffy!" yelled her owner, a pretty lady with curly hair.

"Now look what you've done," Dee Dee groaned.

Fluffy and I sat down to chat while our owners tried to untangle the leashes.

"You have to go to Elm Street," Fluffy barked. "They're filming a movie."

"So?" I barked back. The beautiful homes of Soundview Manor were often used as locations for commercials, TV shows, and even movies.

"They set out a big table of cold cuts on the

**23**

sidewalk for dinner," Fluffy said. "They should be just finishing and I'm sure there'll be leftovers. You must try the roast beef. It's fabulous."

Now that *was* great news. "Thanks for the tip."

By now Dee Dee and Fluffy's owner had finished untangling our leashes. I quickly started to pull Dee Dee toward Elm Street.

"Wordsworth!" Dee Dee tugged back on the leash. "Where are you going? I don't want to go that way!"

Dee Dee may not have wanted to go that way, but I wasn't going to give her any choice. I am an eighty-five-pound basset hound. I have a thick neck, strong legs, and a low center of gravity. If I really want to go somewhere, it takes more than Dee Dee to stop me.

"Oh, well." Dee Dee gave up and started to follow me. "I guess we'll go your way."

Wonderful scents soon began to waft in my direction. First salami, then pastrami, ham, roast beef, Swiss cheese, and cheddar. It smelled like heaven! I started to pull even harder.

"Wordsworth!" Dee Dee cried, holding on to my leash and running to keep up with me. "What's gotten into you?"

It wasn't what had gotten into me. It was what was *going* to get into me. I turned the corner onto Elm Street. Ahead of us, half a dozen trucks and mobile homes lined the street. People were standing around them. Thick black cables ran this way and that across the pavement. Huge lights were shining onto the front yard where the movie was being filmed.

"Gee," Dee Dee said. "Looks like they're making a movie. I didn't know you were interested in movies, Wordsworth."

I wasn't. I was interested in what the movie crew left behind after dinner. Now I could see the table. It was pretty high, which was bad. But it had a tablecloth, which was good. A man and a woman were starting to clear away the leftovers. I knew I had to act fast.

Jumping up, I grabbed the fringe of the tablecloth in my mouth and pulled.

*Clang!* Just as I hoped, a platter of sliced meats tipped over and fell to the street.

"Wordsworth!" Dee Dee cried, trying to pull back on the leash. She didn't have a prayer. I quickly got a mouthful of pastrami. Ummm! It was fabulous!

"I'm really sorry," Dee Dee was saying to the people from the movie company who came around the table to clean up. "It's just that he's so strong. When he really wants something I can't stop him."

"Oh, it's okay," said a man with a black ponytail. "A golden retriever came by a few minutes ago and did the same thing. Besides, this was all leftovers. We were probably gonna throw it out anyway."

In *that* case. I lunged forward again and got a mouthful of the roast beef. Fluffy was right. It was tender, juicy, excellent quality.

**25**

"Stop it, Wordsworth!" Dee Dee yanked the leash as hard as she could. By now the movie people had cleared away all the good stuff. But there were still a few tidbits on the street to lap up.

"What are you filming?" Dee Dee asked the man with the ponytail.

"The exteriors for a movie called *Chain-Saw Baby-Sitter,*" he said. "It's by Alan Roberts."

"The one who makes all the horror movies?" Dee Dee's eyes went wide. "I loved *Toad Serum Killers.* And didn't he do *The Thing from the Cuisinart, Camp Slaughter,* and *The Bride Wore Okra?*"

"Yeah, all of them," the man said. "But just wait until you see this one. The actress who plays the baby-sitter lived in a logging camp for a month. You should see the way she handles that chain saw."

"Cool," Dee Dee said. "When's it coming out?"

"Probably around Christmas," the ponytailed guy said. "We're on a rush schedule. They're supposed to be building the sets back in Hollywood right now. As soon as we finish the exteriors here, we'll go back to California and do the interior scenes. By the way, that's about the biggest basset hound I've ever seen."

"I know," Dee Dee said, stroking my back. "He weighs almost eighty-five pounds, but the doctor says he should be down around sixty."

Don't hold your breath, I thought.

"I like him like that," the guy with the ponytail said. "I mean, he's massive."

I smiled. This was my kind of guy.

"You said his name is Wordsworth?" the guy said.

"Like the poet," said Dee Dee.

"I bet Alan would like to see him," the guy said. "He's really into dogs, especially basset hounds."

Hey, I thought, I could be a star!

"That would be neat," Dee Dee said.

"Alan's gonna be pretty busy for the rest of this week," the guy said. "But you should come back next week. My name's Mike, so just ask for me and I'll take you to meet Alan."

I liked the idea of becoming a movie star. I'd get an agent, and ask for a play-or-pay deal with gross points in the back end. I'd make enough so the Chandlers wouldn't have to worry about money. And I'd have all the roast beef I could eat.

Move over Stallone and Schwarzenegger, I thought. Here comes Wordsworth!

# Seven

**The sound of the front door slamming** early the next morning woke me. I saw Leyland leave the house wearing his blue suit. I remembered he said he was going to the bank to see about money. Then I went back to sleep.

Later Dee Dee took me to Soundview Manor Park. It's a pretty place with stone benches and gazebos on the shores of Bell Island Sound. When I was a puppy I used to enjoy scampering over the rocks by the water and chasing squirrels. Thank goodness that period of my life didn't last long.

"Get the ball, Wordsworth." Dee Dee threw a yellow tennis ball across the grass and unhooked my leash. I looked at her like she was crazy. She didn't really expect me to fetch, did she?

"Don't you want to get in shape?" Dee Dee asked.

I *am* in shape, I thought, and lay down in a nice shady spot.

"Oh, Wordsworth, what *am* I going to do about

you?" Dee Dee asked with a sigh. Then she sat down and put her arms around my neck and gave me a hug. She always gave in.

"That's it, Roy!" a familiar voice shouted behind us. "You can do it!"

Dee Dee and I turned and saw Roy racing toward us across the grass. He was pulling something silvery on a long black string. It was bouncing and dragging on the ground behind him. As he got closer I could see that the silver thing was shaped like a kite.

"Hi, Roy." Dee Dee waved when her brother got close.

"Oh, uh, hi, Dee." He stopped running and wiped some sweat off his forehead. He was huffing and puffing.

"What are you doing?" Dee Dee asked.

"I'm trying to help Dad with his solar-energy-collecting kite," Roy said. "He thinks he can sell it if we can get it to fly."

"How's it going?" Dee Dee asked.

"Not good," Roy replied.

Now Leyland joined us. "Why'd you stop, Roy?"

"I got tired, Dad," Roy said. "I've been dragging this thing around for nearly half an hour."

"Hmmm." Leyland rubbed his chin. "I wonder what the problem is."

"It's too heavy," Roy said.

"But I can't make it any lighter," Leyland said.

"I really don't understand what it's for anyway," Roy said. "I know it's supposed to collect energy from the sun. But then what?"

# Wordsworth and the Cold Cut Catastrophe

"Then it converts the energy into electricity," his father said.

"So?" Roy said.

"So then you'll have electricity," Leyland said.

"Dad, I hate to tell you this," Roy said, "but if I need electricity I can just plug into the wall and get it."

"Not if you're outside," Leyland said.

"Why would I need electricity outside?" Roy asked.

"Suppose you wanted to listen to music?"

"I'd bring a radio with batteries," Roy said.

"With my solar-energy-collecting kite, you wouldn't need batteries," Leyland said.

"But, Dad, it's a lot easier to use batteries than to try and fly a kite that's too heavy," Roy said.

Leyland sat down on a stone bench. His shoulders sagged. "You have a point there, Roy."

"I'm really sorry to shoot down your invention, Dad," Roy said.

Leyland nodded. "No, no, you're right. It's just that this was my last hope for making some money."

"What happened at the bank?" Dee Dee asked.

Leyland stared down at the ground. "They won't give us a loan."

"How come, Dad?" Roy asked.

"They're not convinced that we would pay them back," her father explained.

"Then what are we going to do?" Roy asked.

"I guess we'll have to tighten our belts," Leyland said. "Luckily it's summer and your mother's

**31**

vegetable garden will be coming up soon. We can always eat salad."

"Salad?" Roy made a face that reflected the way I felt.

"You can't feed us salad for two months," Dee Dee protested. "It . . . it won't be good for us."

"Vegetarians eat salads all the time," Leyland said. "It doesn't hurt them."

"Dee Dee and I aren't vegetarians," Roy argued. "We're teenagers."

"Almost," Dee Dee added.

"It could stunt our growth," Roy said.

"Owwwwooooooooo!" I howled. No one seemed to be paying any attention to me.

Dee Dee got the hint and put her arms around me. "What about Wordsworth? Is *he* supposed to eat salad, too?"

"I suppose not," Leyland said. "But he doesn't have to have a lamb chop every night."

"But that's all he eats," Dee Dee protested.

"I think it's only fair that we all share this burden equally," Leyland said. "If we have to eat salad, the least Wordsworth can do is eat dog food."

Dog food? He couldn't be serious. I hadn't touched that stuff since I was three months old.

"Dad, that's mean," Dee Dee complained. "At least let him have a lamb chop once in a while."

"Oh, okay," Leyland said. "He can have a lamb chop once a week."

"Owwwwooooooooo!" I howled in despair.

# Eight

**That night the Chandlers had to make** dinner from things they found in the cupboard. I sat on a nice cool spot on the floor and scratched my ear with my back paw. Janine found a family-size can of baked beans and Flora found a jar of caviar.

"Baked beans and fish eggs?" Dee Dee grimaced.

"I'm sorry, darling," Flora said, "but beggars can't be choosers."

"I remember once spending a whole winter on a boat in the harbor at Copenhagen eating nothing but canned mussels and day-old Danish," Leyland said. He was standing at the sink, wrapping the leaking kitchen faucet with duct tape. A great deal of the Chandlers' house was held together with the thick gray tape.

"I think I've found something!" Roy called. He had crawled into a cabinet under the sink and only his legs stuck out.

Then the phone rang. The Chandlers looked at each other warily.

"Someone's got to answer it," Leyland said.

"Not me," Janine, Dee Dee, and Flora all said at the same time.

Roy backed out of the cabinet and held up a slightly moldy box of Ritz crackers. "Look!"

"Do you think they're still edible?" Flora asked. Meanwhile, the phone continued to ring.

Roy opened the box and looked inside. "Some of them." He looked in my direction. "And the rest we can give to Wordsworth."

Gee, thanks, I thought. I started to scratch the other ear.

*Brrriiinnngggg!* The phone rang insistently.

"Isn't anyone going to answer it?" Roy asked.

Around the kitchen everyone shook their heads.

"What a bunch of chickens," Roy said. He marched over to the phone and answered it. "Hello? Oh, uh, hi, Mr. Pulsky. Uh, sure, he's right here. Yes, sir, right away."

Roy held the phone out toward his father. "It's Mr. Pulsky again."

Leyland shook his head and backed away. "Tell him I'm out."

Roy put his hand over the receiver. "I already told him you're right here."

"Say you made a mistake," Leyland said.

"I can't," Roy said. "He'll know I'm lying."

Leyland sighed and reached for the phone. Once again, we all heard Mr. Pulsky's gruff loud voice.

"But, Mr. Pulsky," Leyland said, "as I told you last night, I have no money at the moment."

Mr. Pulsky growled and barked some more. Finally Leyland hung up the phone, looking pale and shaken again.

"What'd he say?" Janine asked. She had just come from tennis, and was wearing a white polo shirt, shorts, and a white headband.

"The same thing," Leyland replied. "Only he seemed to be a little nastier."

*Briiiinnggg!* The phone began to ring again. Everyone stared nervously at it.

"Oh, come on," Roy said, reaching for it. "You know it won't be that Pulsky guy because he just called." He picked up the phone. "Hello? Oh, uh, yes, sir, he's right here."

Roy held the phone out to his father. "It's for you."

"Mr. Pulsky again?" Leyland asked nervously.

"No, it's a Mr. Pryer, from the Forkit Over Collection Agency," Roy said.

Leyland rolled his eyes and took the phone. We heard another gruff voice demanding money. Once again Leyland explained how he had no money.

Like Mr. Pulsky, Mr. Pryer said he didn't care. After a while Leyland hung up and slumped into a chair. "Those people aren't very nice," he said.

"If they were nice they'd never get you to pay," Janine said.

"We better figure out a way to make some

bucks," Roy said as he poured some moldy Ritz crackers into my food bowl. "I mean, if we eat the baked beans and caviar tonight, that leaves canned asparagus and sardines for tomorrow."

"I've got a baby-sitting job tonight," Janine said.

"Splendid!" Flora looked pleased. "How much will you make, dear?"

When Janine told them, both Flora and Leyland looked surprised.

"That much?" Leyland said. "Perhaps we should all get baby-sitting jobs."

"Don't you think it would be a little strange if you or Mom showed up to baby-sit?" Roy asked.

Flora and Leyland gave each other questioning looks. "I'm afraid he's probably right, dear," Flora said with a sigh.

"Then I know!" Leyland said excitedly. "Perhaps we should open one of those places where people bring the children to us."

"Like a day-care center?" Dee Dee asked.

"Yes, precisely," her father said. "We've got a big house. There's certainly enough room."

"I do love the sound of little feet scampering about the house," Flora said.

Dee Dee, Roy, and Janine gave each other wary looks. I knew what they were thinking. The house was downright dangerous. The stairs banister was held together with duct tape, floorboards were missing here and there, and every so often a large slab of plaster would crash down from the ceiling. A baby would be lucky to survive.

"I think we'd better come up with some *other* way to make money," Janine said.

"I know!" Roy gasped. "You know how our house is filled with old junk?"

Leyland and Flora looked surprised. "I beg your pardon, Roy."

"Well, er, I mean, it's not junk actually," Roy corrected himself. "But it's stuff we don't really need."

"I'm not sure I even agree with *that,*" Leyland said.

"Oh, come on, Dad, what about that old rocking horse in the basement?" Roy said.

"I'm saving that for you when you have children," Flora said.

"What about all the old tennis rackets?" Roy asked.

"We have them for guests who want to play at the club," Leyland said.

"When was the last time we had guests?" Dee Dee asked.

Not in *my* lifetime, I thought. I stretched out my front paws and arched my back.

"We might, someday," Flora said.

"Just what is your point, Roy?" Leyland asked.

"We should have a tag sale," Roy said.

"That's a great idea!" Dee Dee said eagerly. "There's tons of stuff we could sell."

"We could put an ad in the paper," Janine said excitedly.

"If it's a really hot day, we could sell lemonade to everyone who came," Dee Dee said.

"And hot dogs and hamburgers, too," Roy added.

"Oh, come on, Mom, Dad," Dee Dee begged. "Let's do it. I bet we'll make a ton of money. Then we'll be able to pay Mr. Pulsky and Mr. Pryer and everyone else."

Flora and Leyland gave each other uncertain looks, but finally agreed. Everyone except Dee Dee left the kitchen. Of course, I hadn't touched those disgusting crackers in my bowl.

"Moldy crackers." Dee Dee shook her head and emptied the bowl in the garbage. "What do they think you are, Wordsworth, a garbage disposal?"

It was so nice that someone understood.

Dee Dee opened the freezer and reached way in back, behind the ice tray. She pulled out something wrapped in tin foil.

"I hid a few of these for you," she said, unwrapping the foil. "In case of an emergency."

From out of the foil she took a frozen lamb chop and stuck it in the microwave.

"I know you like them broiled, but then everyone will smell the smoke," she explained. "So I have to cook it in the microwave."

I barked in agreement. A microwaved lamb chop tends to be a little tough, but it is certainly better than moldy Ritz crackers.

# Nine

**I spent the rest of the week day-**dreaming about my starring role in the new Alan Roberts movie, *Attack of the Killer Tabby Cats from Mars.* Of course, I would play the hero who saves my canine cousins.

Thanks to Janine's baby-sitting job and some lawns cut by Roy, the Chandlers had just enough money for food. Somehow Dee Dee managed to sneak me a microwaved lamb chop every night. I didn't ask where she was getting the cash for them, but I think it came from the money she'd been saving for a new plastic horse.

A large bag of dog food did appear in the kitchen broom closet. Each evening Dee Dee would pour some of the yucky-looking brown pellets into my bowl. But after dinner she would wait until everyone left the kitchen. Then she would pour them back into the bag and give me a lamb chop instead.

It was a difficult week for the Chandlers. They tried to prepare for the tag sale, but they couldn't decide what to sell. Flora couldn't bear to part with the lamp her aunt Matilda had given her. Leyland wouldn't give up the skis he hadn't used in fifteen years. Dee Dee suddenly felt sentimental about her old dolls. Janine refused to part with her collection of autographed baseballs. And Roy decided to keep his comic books because they might be worth a fortune someday.

Finally it was the night before the tag sale. The issue was brought up for discussion at dinner.

"We can't really have a tag sale if we don't have anything to sell," Roy pointed out.

"He's right," Flora said. "Maybe we should cancel it."

"We can't cancel it, Mom," Janine said. "We put an ad in the local paper, remember? People have even come up to me in the street and asked what we were going to sell."

"We can still sell lemonade and hot dogs," Dee Dee said.

"I think they're going to be disappointed if they come for a tag sale and all we have is food," Roy said.

"Roy's right," said Leyland. "Each of us is going to have to come up with something to sell. Now think."

"I know," Janine said. "I have this collection of every bottle of perfume any boy has given me since fifth grade. I never wear any of it. Maybe we could sell that."

# Wordsworth and the Cold Cut Catastrophe

"Good idea," Leyland said.

After dinner, each member of the family went off to a different part of the house to decide what they were going to sell. Only Dee Dee stayed behind in the kitchen. She looked sad.

"Bad news, Wordsworth," she said. "I've used up all my savings. There are no more lamb chops."

I looked at those awful brown pellets in my food bowl. Then I looked back at Dee Dee. She *had* to be kidding.

"I'm serious," she said as if she'd read my mind. "Tonight it's dog food or nothing."

I gave her the saddest look I could.

"Please don't look at me like that," Dee Dee begged, petting my head. "There's nothing I can do."

Not true, I thought. If she *really* cared about me she could have robbed the meat counter at the local food store. I trudged slowly to the sliding screen door—patched with duct tape, of course—and lay down.

Dee Dee got on her hands and knees and started to pet my side. I rolled over on my back and let her scratch my stomach. "Oh, Wordsworth, I hate to see you so sad. I really do. You know what I'm going to do? I'm going to sell all my dolls tomorrow. And I'm going to keep all the money and just buy lamb chops for you."

I knew it would be a terrible sacrifice for her.

But hey, a dog has to eat.

# Ten

**That night I kept waking up. Usually**
I can sleep from dinner until eight or nine in the
morning. But usually I have a lamb chop in my
stomach. That night my stomach was empty. The
scent of that horrid dog food hung in the dark
kitchen air. No, I told myself, don't eat it. If I ate
that stuff they'd never feed me a lamb chop again.

Around midnight I heard the sound of a tree rustling
outside. That was odd, because there was no wind. I
heard the rustling sound again. Raccoons sometimes
came around at night, looking through the garbage cans
for leftovers. But you didn't hear them in trees.

"*Hey, look out!*" someone whispered outside.

"*Keep your voice down!*" whispered someone else.

Burglars! I was on my feet instantly. We'd never had
burglars before. Dee Dee always said I was an exceptional
guard dog. Now was my chance to prove her right.

But how?

# Wordsworth and the Cold Cut Catastrophe

Barking loudly seemed like a good idea. Surely that would chase the burglars away. But wasn't that what an *average* guard dog would do? An exceptional guard dog would do more.

An exceptional guard dog would help *catch* the burglars!

I scampered out of the kitchen and up the stairs as fast as my sturdy legs would carry me. It had been a long time since I'd run up the stairs. They seemed a lot longer than I remembered, and my tummy kept bumping on them. I even had to stop and catch my breath for a moment.

Finally I made it into Dee Dee's bedroom. In the darkness I could see Dee Dee under her blanket, fast asleep in the middle of her large old bed. I hopped up on my hind legs and tried to reach her with my front paws, but she was too far away!

Next, I tried to jump up on the bed itself, but I couldn't get enough spring from my hind legs. That was odd. I used to be able to jump up on beds all the time.

Not being able to reach her, I yipped and yelped softly. I was afraid of barking too loudly. That might scare the burglars away and make me look like nothing more than an average guard dog.

"Yip, yip . . . Yelp, yelp . . ." I felt like an idiot making those sounds. Dee Dee didn't budge. I remembered Leyland once saying that she slept like a log. Boy, he wasn't kidding!

Next I grabbed the blanket between my teeth and pulled it off her. Dee Dee rolled over and grunted, but didn't wake up.

If I didn't do something quick, those burglars were going to get into the house!

So I said the first thing that came into my head. "Dee Dee! Get up!"

"Huh?" Dee Dee sat straight up in bed. She rubbed her eyes and looked around in the dark. "Who said that?"

It occurred to me that I had. Since when did I know how to talk?

Dee Dee turned on the lamp beside her bed. She squinted in the bright light. "Is someone in here?"

I got up on my hind legs and looked over the bed.

"Oh, it's you." She smiled. "I just had the weirdest dream. I could have sworn someone told me to get up."

"Yip, yip . . . Yelp, yelp." I tried to act like a dog again. I wasn't sure I wanted anyone to know I could talk.

Dee Dee yawned. "Sorry, Wordsworth. It's the middle of the night. I can't play with you. Go back to sleep."

Before I could stop her, she pulled her blanket off the floor, then reached over to the lamp and shut it off.

*She thought I wanted to play!*

"Yip, yip . . . yelp, yelp!"

"Please, Wordsworth," Dee Dee muttered. "I want to go back to sleep."

There were burglars outside and Dee Dee wanted to go back to sleep. This was no good.

"You have to get up, Dee Dee," I said.

The light burst on again. Dee Dee sat up in bed. "Who said that?" She looked at me. "Is someone in here, Wordsworth?"

"Just me," I said.

# Eleven

**"Ah!" Dee Dee's mouth opened as if she** was going to scream.

"Shush!" I put a paw to my lips.

She stared at me with wide eyes. "You can talk!"

"You have to be quiet or you'll scare the burglars away," I said. I liked my voice. It sounded deep and refined.

"What are you talking about?" she asked.

"The burglars," I said.

Dee Dee kept staring at me. "I can't believe this."

"That there are burglars, or that I can talk?" I asked.

"Both. But more that you can talk."

"Believe me, I'm surprised, too," I said. "But we can talk about that later. Right now we have to catch those burglars."

Dee Dee was still staring at me.

"Come on, there's no time to lose," I said.

**47**

She pinched herself. "Ouch!"

"This isn't a dream," I said. "But it may be a nightmare if we don't do something about those burglars."

"Where are they?" she asked.

"Outside, in a tree," I said.

"In a tree?" Dee Dee frowned. "What are they doing in a tree?"

Hmmm. I hadn't thought of that. Why would burglars be in a tree? "I don't know."

"Will you please explain to me how you learned to talk?" Dee Dee said.

"I'm not sure I can," I said. "But I do know that this isn't the time. There are burglars outside, Dee Dee. There really are."

"Which tree?" she asked.

"The tree that goes up past Janine's bedroom window," I said.

All at once Dee Dee smiled.

"What's so funny?" I asked.

"You wouldn't understand," she said, sliding out of bed and pulling on her robe.

"What do you mean, I wouldn't understand?" I asked, following her out of her room. "I can talk, can't I?"

"Yeah, but this is different," she said, heading quickly down the stairs.

"What is this?" I bounced down the stairs behind her, feeling completely insulted. "You think just because I'm a dog I won't understand?"

Dee Dee didn't answer. She stopped in the

kitchen and searched through the drawers until she found a flashlight. "Now follow me and stay quiet," she whispered, sliding the kitchen door open.

I followed her out into the cool night air. "Are you sure this is safe?" I whispered.

"Shhh!"

In the dark, Dee Dee tiptoed over the dew-covered grass. I couldn't understand why she had taken the flashlight if she didn't intend to use it.

We came to the tree. High above us, I could see dark shadows in the branches outside Janine's bedroom window. Dee Dee raised the flashlight and flicked it on.

Two boys stared down at us with startled looks on their faces. It was Adam Pickney and his friend Joseph, the one with the long brown hair.

"Hi, guys," Dee Dee said with a smirk. "Looking for something?"

"Chill out, Dee Dee," Adam Pickney muttered, and started to climb down.

"Gee, Adam," Dee Dee said, "I wonder why you'd be sitting in a tree outside Janine's window in the middle of the night?"

"Just shut up, okay?"

But Dee Dee had no intention of doing that. "Janine!" she called. "Oh, Janine!"

"Hey, can it!" Adam sputtered.

Janine's window slid open and she stuck her head out. "Who's there?" she said.

"It's me," Dee Dee said, shining the flashlight on Adam and his friend. "Look what I found in the tree outside your window."

Janine's mouth fell open. "Why you!" She disappeared from the window.

"Uh-oh, better skate!" Adam gasped, and started to climb down the tree even faster. Suddenly he stopped. "Darn!"

"What's wrong?" Joseph asked.

"My shirt's stuck on a branch!"

While Adam struggled to free his shirt from the branch, Janine returned to her window. In each hand she held three or four small glass bottles. She turned them upside down and liquid began to pour out of them.

"Gross!" Adam shouted.

"What the . . . ?" gasped Joseph.

"She's dumping perfume on us!" Adam cried.

He was right. The air was suddenly filled with a dozen strong flowery scents.

"Guess I won't have as much perfume as I thought to sell tomorrow," Janine said from her window.

"I'm sure Dad will understand," Dee Dee called back.

By the time Adam and Joseph got to the ground, they reeked of perfume.

"That'll teach you to climb up trees where you don't belong," Dee Dee said.

"Why you . . ." Adam made a fist and stepped toward her.

# Wordsworth and the Cold Cut Catastrophe

Dee Dee looked down at me. "Wordsworth?"

"Uh . . . grrrrr," I growled.

Adam stopped and stared at me, then at Dee Dee. "Did he say, uh?"

"No, he said, grrrrr," Dee Dee said.

"I thought he said, uh," Adam said.

"Maybe he said, uh, grrrr," said Dee Dee.

"No, he said uh like a person says uh," Adam insisted.

"Look, you better get out of here before I call the police and say uh, there are two burglars in my backyard," Dee Dee said.

Adam and his friend backed away. "I'll get you for this," he threatened. "And I'll get your dog, too."

At least he didn't say, *little* dog, I thought proudly.

# Twelve

**"Are they gone?"** Janine asked from the window.

"Yup." Dee Dee nodded.

"Thanks," her big sister said.

"Anytime," Dee Dee said.

Dee Dee and I went inside. I went over to my doggy bed and lay down. All the excitement had tired me. Dee Dee got down on her hands and knees and began to stroke me. I started to drift off to sleep.

"Uh, Wordsworth?" she said.

"Hmmm?"

"I think we better talk."

I yawned. "Can't it wait until the morning?"

"I don't think so."

"But I'm tired," I said.

"Wordsworth," Dee Dee said firmly. "Dogs are not supposed to talk."

"Why not?" I asked.

"Because they're not," she said.

"People bark," I said.

Dee Dee blinked. It was obvious she'd never considered that.

"I'd really like to get some rest," I said, and yawned again. Dee Dee kept petting me.

"Wordsworth, don't you understand how amazing this is?" she asked. "I mean, how did you learn to talk?"

"Uh, 'Sesame Street'?"

She frowned. "I'm serious."

"I really don't know," I said. "I mean, I've been listening to all of you talk for years. I'd have to be an idiot not to have learned a few phrases."

Dee Dee stared at me in wonder.

"Please don't look at me like that," I said. "It makes me feel like I'm in a zoo."

"Do any of your friends talk?" she asked.

"Of course, we talk all the time."

"I meant, do they speak English?"

"I don't know," I said. "I never asked."

"This is amazing," Dee Dee said. "You're probably the only dog in the world who can talk. You could go on talk shows and be in movies! You could be rich!"

My ears perked up. She was right. I could have all the lamb chops I wanted! And cold cuts! I could have a heated doggy bed! And if I got really rich, I could have my very own, full-time, personal scratcher!

"Oh, no, wait a minute!" Dee Dee gasped. "You know what will happen if people find out you can talk? Scientists will want to study you. They'll cut open your brain and look inside."

"You think?" I asked with a cringe.

"Sure," Dee Dee said. "It happens in the movies all the time. Remember *E.T.* and *Splash!* and *The Flight of the Navigator?* As soon as they find out you're different or unusual, scientists want to look at your insides."

That didn't sound like fun.

"Oh, Wordsworth!" Dee Dee wrapped her arms around my neck and hugged me. "I love you. I don't want them to take you away. Please don't tell anyone you can talk, please! It has to be our secret."

"Dee Dee?" a voice said.

Dee Dee and I both looked up, startled. Janine was standing in the doorway, wearing the oversize white T-shirt she slept in each night.

"Who was that talking?" Janine asked with a yawn.

"Uh, no one."

Janine craned her neck to look around the kitchen. "I heard you talking to someone. Who's here?"

"Uh, oh, I wasn't talking to *someone*," Dee Dee said. "I was just talking to Wordsworth."

I stared at her in astonishment. Didn't she just insist that we shouldn't tell anyone?

Janine smiled. "I'm sure you two have a lot to say to each other. But it's really late and you should get to bed, okay?"

# Wordsworth and the Cold Cut Catastrophe

"All right," Dee Dee said, giving me a wink. "Just let me say good night to Wordsworth and I'll be right up."

Janine left the kitchen and Dee Dee smiled at me.

"See?" she whispered. "I can talk to you all I want. They're used to that. You just can't talk to me, okay?"

"It doesn't seem fair," I grumbled.

"I know," Dee Dee said sympathetically. "But would you rather end up in some laboratory with scientists studying little slivers of your brain under a microscope?"

She had a good point.

# Thirteen

~~~~

**The next day was the tag sale. At 7:30** in the morning, I was awakened by the sound of knocking on the front door. Of course, no one in the house was up at that hour, so no one answered.

But the knocking continued steadily for ten minutes. Finally I heard a bedroom door open on the second floor. The stairs creaked as Leyland came down. He was pulling his blue robe closed and mumbling to himself.

"Who in the world? Don't they know it's still the middle of the night?"

He opened the door. A man and woman were standing outside. They were both rather plump.

"Is this the place with the tag sale?" the man asked.

"Why, yes, but didn't the ad say it would start in the afternoon?" Leyland replied.

"Oh, George and I never pay attention to that," said the woman, stepping past Leyland and into the house. "By then all the good stuff is gone. Say, neat old house. I bet you just moved in and you want to clear out all this old junk."

Leyland frowned. "Why would you think we just moved in?"

"Because the place is such a wreck," the woman said. "You just bought it and now you're going to fix it up, right?"

"Actually, my wife and I have lived here for fifteen years," Leyland said.

"Oh, uh, sorry," the woman mumbled sheepishly.

"Anyway," said George, "Mildred and I were wondering if we could get a preview."

"Preview?" Leyland repeated, bewildered.

"Of what you have for sale," Mildred said, wandering into the living room.

"Well, uh, we haven't quite made up our minds," Leyland said.

"Wow, that's the biggest dachshund I ever saw." George pointed at me.

*Dachshund!* I'd never been so insulted in my life!

"Sorry, he's a basset hound," Leyland said.

"Oh, George!" Mildred called from the living room. "Look what I found."

George hurried past Leyland into the living room. Mildred was standing by the fireplace.

"Solid brass fireplace tools," she said.

George turned to Leyland. "What do you think you'll ask for these?"

"Well, I don't think we planned to sell them, actually," Leyland said. "They've been in my wife's family for generations."

"Too bad." George shook his head. "I would've given you three bucks for the set."

"And look at this clock!" Mildred said, admiring a large gold clock on the fireplace mantel. "Is this really gold?"

"Why, yes," Leyland said.

"I'll bet this goes back a long way."

"In fact it does," Leyland said proudly. "It's nearly three hundred years old."

"Take five bucks for it?" George asked.

"Sorry," Leyland said. "I'm almost certain that won't be for sale. It's a family heirloom."

George scratched his head and looked around. "Maybe you ought to tell us what will be on sale. We've got a pretty busy schedule, you know. We can't stay all day."

"I understand," Leyland said, showing them toward the door. "That's why I think you ought to come back later."

"Well, okay," George said. "Just remember, if you change your mind about those fireplace tools, I got first dibs."

"I'll definitely remember," Leyland said, opening the door for them.

George went through, but Mildred paused and gazed around the inside of the house.

# Wordsworth and the Cold Cut Catastrophe

"You know what this place would be perfect for?" she said. "A bed-and-breakfast."

"I beg your pardon?" Leyland said.

"A bed-and-breakfast," Mildred said. "You know. People come and stay. They pay you and you give them a bed-and-breakfast. They love old places like this. And you're so close to the park and Bell Island Sound. You could make a fortune."

"Uh, I'll be sure to remember that," Leyland said, closing the door behind her.

"So what do you think, Wordsworth?" he said with a wry smile. "A bed-and-breakfast?"

Sleep and eat? Sounded good to me.

# Fourteen

**Leyland told me to growl at anyone**
else who came to the door. Then he went back to bed.
Unfortunately, no one got much sleep that morning. A
steady parade of early birds banged on the front door. I
growled at the first few, but then I got bored with it.

By nine A.M. the whole family was standing at the
front door. Outside dozens of people were milling
around the front yard, waiting for the tag sale to begin.

"What should we do?" Leyland asked.

"Maybe they'd like some coffee," Flora said. "I
could make them a pot."

"Great idea," Roy said. "We'll sell it."

"Sell coffee?" Flora scowled.

"This is a tag sale, Mom," Roy tried to explain.
"You can sell *anything*."

"Anything?"

"Look." Roy opened the front closet and pulled
out a pair of white, fuzzy earmuffs.

"My old earmuffs," Janine said.

"Still want them?" Roy asked.

Janine shook her head.

"Be right back," Roy said. He went outside. In less than a minute he came back inside with two quarters and gave them to Janine. "See?"

"Why would anyone want earmuffs in the middle of the summer?" Flora asked.

"They don't," Roy said. "They just like to buy things. Dad, you know that old radio in the basement? You still want it?"

"No," Leyland said. "It's broken. It hasn't worked in years."

"Watch." Roy went downstairs and came back with the radio. He went outside and returned a few moments later with a dollar.

"See how easy it is?" he said.

"I have about a hundred pairs of worn-out tennis shoes," Janine said, hurrying up the stairs.

"I'll get my dolls," said Dee Dee, following her.

"Do you think they'd want old paintbrushes?" Flora asked.

"Definitely," said Roy. He turned to Leyland. "Come on, Dad, there must be something you can sell."

"I can't think of what," Leyland replied. "All I've got are dozens of inventions. I've never been able to sell any of them."

"You never tried a tag sale," Roy said.

# Fifteen

—⦉⦊—

**For the next two hours, the Chandlers** sold every piece of useless junk they owned. I stretched out on the front porch and watched while they discovered that for the right price they could sell almost anything. Jigsaw puzzles with missing pieces sold for a quarter. A chair with a broken leg sold for two dollars and someone even bought a cracked mirror!

For a while it looked like they were going to make lots of money. Then a large white car pulled up and Charles Pickney, the mayor of Soundview, got out. Mayor Pickney was Adam's father and the Chandlers' next-door neighbor. He was a round man who wore pink polo shirts and bright plaid pants. His white leather shoes smelled of grass, so I knew he'd been playing golf.

"Wanna buy some broken golf tees, Mayor Pickney?" Roy asked eagerly.

"I certainly do not!" Mayor Pickney huffed. "Where is your father, young man?"

Dee Dee and I glanced at each other. I think we both thought the same thing—that Mayor Pickney was angry because Janine had dumped perfume on Adam the night before.

Leyland came out of the house with a box filled with old paint cans. "Hello, Charles, need some paint?"

"No," Mayor Pickney snapped. "And if I did, I'd buy it at the paint store."

"I'll give you a better price," Leyland said. He'd really gotten into the tag sale spirit.

"I'm not interested!" Mayor Pickney was clearly upset. He swung his arm around. "Look around, Chandler. What do you see?"

Leyland looked around. "I see cars and people."

"That's right. Here, in beautiful Soundview Manor, you see cars lining both sides of the street. And some of them are parked with their wheels on *my* lawn!"

Mayor Pickney was very serious about his lawn.

"And you see people," Mayor Pickney sputtered. "Strangers wandering around our lovely neighborhood. And some of them—"

"Are stepping on your lawn," Leyland finished the sentence for him.

"That's right!" Mayor Pickney's face turned red. He was really mad.

"I bet he had a bad game of golf this morning," Dee Dee whispered to me.

I almost replied that he did seem teed off, but then I remembered I wasn't supposed to speak. Much less make puns . . .

"I'll ask them to stay off your lawn," Leyland said.

"That's not the point," Mayor Pickney fumed. "The point is that once again you have turned this beautiful neighborhood into a carnival and an eyesore."

"It's not as if we have a tag sale every day," Leyland said.

"No, but you live here every day," Mayor Pickney said. "Your house is a shambles. Your lawn is a disgrace! And your children!"

"What about my children?" Leyland hardly cared about the house and the lawn. But he'd never allow anyone to say anything mean about his children.

"Are you aware that your daughter poured perfume on Adam last night?"

Leyland looked surprised. "Why would she do that?"

"I suggest you ask her," Mayor Pickney said.

Leyland looked around for Janine, who was selling lemonade.

"Janine, could you come here for a moment?"

Janine came over and Leyland asked her if it was true.

"You bet," Janine said.

"Why would you pour perfume on Adam?" Leyland asked.

"Because he was up in the tree outside my window in the middle of the night, trying to look in," Janine replied.

"That's not what Adam told me," Mayor Pickney sputtered. "He said you lured him onto your property and then did it."

"Then you should ask him how he tore his shirt on a tree branch and why his pants probably have sap on them," Janine replied.

Mayor Pickney's face turned redder and he glared at Leyland. "Are you aware that it is illegal to have a garage sale in Soundview Manor without a permit?"

"Why no, I wasn't," Leyland said.

Mayor Pickney spun around and marched back to his car. He got inside and made a phone call on his car phone. Then he drove off with a screech of tires.

"I think we're going to have a problem," Dee Dee whispered to me.

She was right. A few moments later a black-and-white Village of Soundview police car pulled up. A policeman got out.

"Are you Mr. Chandler?" he asked Leyland.

"Yes."

"Do you have a tag-sale permit?"

"Uh, no."

"Then I'm afraid I'm going to have to issue you a citation and insist that you stop immediately," the police officer said. He opened a pad and started to write out a ticket.

Leyland turned to the rest of us. "All right, everyone, we have to stop now."

"But it's not fair," Roy protested.

"Do as I say, Roy."

"Here you are, Mr. Chandler," the police officer said, handing him the ticket.

Leyland looked down at it and his jaw dropped. "That's quite a large fine."

"I'm sorry, sir," the police officer apologized. "It's the village law."

Leyland shook his head sadly. Janine and Flora started to carry all the unsold junk back into the house. Then Roy came over.

"You sure you want to sell the car, Dad?" he asked.

"Huh?" Leyland looked surprised. Down at the curb, a tow-truck operator was hooking up the family car. The Chandlers owned a large old convertible. The top was patched with duct tape. Duct tape also held the headlights in place where the metal fenders had rusted away.

Leyland waved to Flora and Janine. "Did one of you sell the car?"

They shook their heads. Leyland started down toward the curb and the rest of us followed. A large man wearing a greasy olive uniform was winching up the front end of the car. He was chewing on the butt of an unlit cigar. He smelled of oil and tobacco.

"Excuse me, sir, but why are you taking our car?" Leyland asked.

"I got court papers," the man said. He handed Leyland a bunch of thin pink sheets with typing on them.

Leyland took out his reading glasses and studied the papers.

"What's it say, Dad?" Roy asked.

"It appears that they've gone to court and gotten permission to take the car," Leyland said.

"Because we owe money?" Janine asked.

Leyland nodded.

"But we've got lots of money now," Roy said.

"Yes," Leyland said, reaching into his pocket. "Perhaps we can pay you whatever we owe."

"Sorry, bud, my job ain't to collect money," the man said. "It's to collect cars."

We watched helplessly as the man hoisted the car up and drove it away. The people who'd come to the tag sale got in their cars and drove away, too. I looked across to the Pickneys' house and saw Mayor Pickney standing on his front walk. His fat arms were crossed and he was smiling.

# Sixteen

⚬⚬⚬⚬

**No one looked happy at dinner that** evening.

"Hey, come on," Roy said. "At least we made some money before the police stopped the tag sale."

"Most of it will go toward the ticket and getting the car back," Leyland said.

"I suppose there's no point in trying to have another tag sale," Dee Dee said.

"It did seem to make Mayor Pickney awfully mad," Flora agreed.

"So why should you care?" Janine asked. "Mayor Pickney is a stupid, shallow man who cares more about his lawn than he does about other people."

"But he's still our neighbor," Flora reminded her. "We must stay on good terms."

"Why?" Roy asked. "That creep Adam climbed up a tree and tried to look into Janine's window last night."

"Well . . . " Flora smiled weakly. "Boys will be boys."

"How'd you like it if I did something like that?" Roy asked.

"That's ridiculous, Roy," Leyland said. "It's not the way you've been brought up."

"Well, how come it's okay for Adam Pickney and not for me?" Roy asked.

"It's not okay for Adam Pickney," Flora said. "But we must be forgiving of others."

"I don't see why." Janine pouted. "The Pickneys don't seem very forgiving of us."

All this talk made me impatient. I knew that Dee Dee had snuck off to the store after the tag sale. She'd bought half a dozen fresh lamb chops with the money from her dolls. I was also starving. It had been two days since I'd eaten. But Dee Dee couldn't cook a lamb chop until everyone finished dinner and left the kitchen.

"Grrrooowww." I let out a sort of half growl, half groan.

"What's with him?" Roy asked.

"He's hungry," Dee Dee said.

"Why doesn't he eat some dog food," Roy said, pointing at my bowl, which was still full of those awful brown pellets.

"He will," Dee Dee said.

"What's he waiting for?" Janine asked.

"Uh, he doesn't like to eat until everyone leaves the kitchen," Dee Dee said.

# Wordsworth and the Cold Cut Catastrophe

The rest of the family gave her strange looks.

"You know what's weird?" said Roy. "I haven't seen Wordsworth eat anything since we switched from lamb chops to dog food."

Dee Dee and I exchanged a nervous glance.

"So, uh, what *are* we going to do about money?" Dee Dee asked, quickly changing the topic.

That's when I remembered what George and Mildred had said that morning.

"Groof! Groof!" I jumped up and ran toward the front door.

"What's gotten into him?" Leyland asked.

"Maybe I should go see," Dee Dee said.

I waited for Dee Dee by the front door.

"What's going on?" she whispered as she bent down and scratched me on the head.

I stretched up and pretended to lick her ear. "Mention a bed-and-breakfast," I whispered back.

"What?" Dee Dee frowned.

"It's when people come and stay for the night and you give them breakfast."

"Why would we do that?" Dee Dee asked.

"Because they'll pay," I said.

"Pay to stay *here* and have breakfast? Why?"

"People love to walk in the park and be near Bell Island Sound," I said.

"You really think?" Dee Dee asked.

"That's what the early birds said this morning," I said.

"Dee Dee?" Flora called from the kitchen. "Are you all right?"

"Yes, Mom," Dee Dee yelled. Then she said to me, "I guess we better go back."

We went back into the kitchen. I lay down on the floor.

"What was it?" Leyland asked.

"Nothing," Dee Dee said. "Know what I think? Maybe we should turn our house into a bed-and-breakfast."

Roy and Janine looked at her like she was crazy.

"What an interesting idea," Flora said. "It sounds so . . . so British. What do you think, Leyland?"

"Well, it is interesting that Dee Dee should mention it," Leyland said. "Because some people this morning mentioned the same thing."

"I think we should do it!" Flora clasped her hands together in an excited way.

"I suppose it's worth considering," Leyland said.

Now that they'd hit on something new, dinner went quickly. Everyone did their own dishes and left, leaving only Dee Dee and me.

"Finally!" I said with a sigh. I got up and went over to the freezer while Dee Dee got out a lamb chop.

"Shhh!" Dee Dee pressed her finger to her lips. "I don't want anyone to hear you."

"Oh, go on," I said. "You know they're all off doing—"

# Wordsworth and the Cold Cut Catastrophe

I didn't have time to finish the sentence before I heard two sets of footsteps. Janine and Roy came back into the kitchen.

"Were you talking to someone again?" Janine asked, looking around.

"Oh, uh, just to Wordsworth," Dee Dee said, giving me a sly wink.

"I'm starting to worry about you, Dee Dee," said Roy. "You spend more time talking to that dog than you do talking to other people."

"Maybe he's more interesting than other people," Dee Dee said.

I couldn't have agreed more.

Janine rolled her eyes. "You are weird. Now, what's this about a bed-and-breakfast?"

"I just thought it might be a good way to make some money," Dee Dee said with a shrug.

"People pay to stay here?" Roy shook his head. "I think you've got it backward, Dee Dee. I think *we'd* have to pay *them*."

"How do you know what a bed-and-breakfast is anyway?" Janine asked.

"Uh . . ." Dee Dee glanced nervously at me. "I saw it on TV."

"Well, forget it," Roy said. "No one's gonna want to stay here. And if they did, who'd cook them breakfast?"

"I will," Dee Dee said.

Janine and Roy looked at each other.

"The only thing you know how to cook are lamb chops," Roy said.

"Look, Dee Dee," Janine said. "All we're trying to say is this is serious. We know that Mom and Dad mean well, but they're off in their own world. So it's up to us to make some money. I'm baby-sitting and Roy's cutting lawns. It would be really helpful if you could contribute, too."

Dee Dee gave me another look. This one made me a little nervous.

"So what do you think you could do?" Roy asked.

"Uh, take Wordsworth out for a walk," she said.

# Seventeen

**Outside, Dee Dee tugged gently on my** leash. "Let's go to the park."

"What about my lamb chop?" I asked.

"You'll have to wait."

"But I'm hungry," I said as we crossed the street and started down a path into the park.

"Don't be such a baby." Dee Dee sounded annoyed.

"What's with you?" I asked.

"Shh!" Dee Dee nodded ahead and I saw Cody and her owner coming toward us on the path.

"Taking an after-dinner stroll?" Cody barked.

"Yes, only I haven't had dinner," I barked back.

"Bummer."

We passed each other. Dee Dee and I strolled under a thick stand of trees. She started to talk to me again. "I've been thinking, Wordsworth. Maybe we should let people know you can talk. We could go on

TV and make a fortune. Then my parents would have money to pay their bills."

"But you said scientists will cut up my brain," I said.

"Some of it," Dee Dee said. "But maybe they'd leave enough so that you could still talk."

"Uh, no thanks," I said.

"But my parents are in big trouble, Wordsworth," Dee Dee said.

"Believe me, I feel bad for them," I said. "But I bet they wouldn't let their brains be sliced up for me."

"If they don't find a way to make money, I may have to do it," Dee Dee said. "I don't see any other choice."

"I'm sorry, Dee Dee," I said. "I know your parents have a big problem. But I won't give up my brain. If you tell people I can talk, I'll just act like a dog and bark. Everyone'll think you're—"

Suddenly someone swung out of the tree in front of us and landed on the path. It was Adam Pickney!

"Ahh!" Dee Dee let out a frightened yelp, but Adam ignored her and pointed at me.

"This time *I know* I heard him talk," he said.

"You scared me," Dee Dee gasped, pressing her hands against her chest.

"How does he do it?" Adam asked.

"I don't know what you're talking about," Dee Dee said. A couple of Adam's grungy friends climbed down from the tree.

**76**

# Wordsworth and the Cold Cut Catastrophe

"Don't you ever get tired of hanging around in trees?" Dee Dee asked.

"Drop dead," Adam said.

"What's goin' on, dude?" his long-haired friend Joseph asked.

"I heard this dog talk." Adam crouched down in front of me. "Say something, Heavy Sausage."

I was tempted to tell him what a jerk he was, but instead I just barked.

"You're faking, you dumb dog," Adam said.

"Whoa, Adam," said Joseph. "You're saying this mutt talks?"

"Yeah."

"I think Adam's flipped," Dee Dee told Joseph.

Adam's friends grinned.

"I'm telling you, he was saying stuff," Adam insisted. "You know what this dog would be worth if we could get him to talk?"

Adam's friends looked at each other and winked.

"I think your brain's a little fried, dude," Joseph said.

"Yeah, Adam, the only talking dog I ever saw was Goofy," said another one.

"Naw, what about Lady and the Tramp?"

"Oh, yeah. And Inspector Hound."

"Maybe Adam think's he's in Toon Town."

His friends nudged each other and chuckled.

"Will you guys shut up?" Adam snapped, straightening up and pointing his finger at Dee Dee.

"I'm gonna get proof. And then I'm gonna sell it to *America's Weirdest Videos.* Your dog's gonna make me rich."

"You're crazy," Dee Dee said. Then she turned to me. "Come on, Wordsworth, let's get out of here."

We left the park and walked along the street. Dee Dee looked around to make sure no one could hear us.

"From now on, we have to be really careful," she whispered. "If Adam can prove you can talk, who knows what he'll do!"

That was something to worry about. But I quickly forgot about Adam when the scent of something wonderful drifted my way. *Pastrami!*

I started to pull on the leash.

"Wordsworth!" Dee Dee cried. "Where are you going?"

I didn't answer. All I could think about was pastrami, and salami, and that delicious roast beef.

"Answer me, Wordsworth," Dee Dee said.

"This'll teach you to skip my dinner," I grunted, straining against the leash. Suddenly I lurched forward. I'd yanked the leash out of Dee Dee's hand!

Full speed ahead!

"Wordsworth!" Dee Dee yelled behind me as I started to run.

I turned the corner onto Elm. There it was! Heaven! Mecca! The film crew's cold-cuts table!

I ran up to the table. I was just about to give the

tablecloth a good yank when someone said, "Hey, look who's here."

I looked up and saw Mike, the man with the black ponytail.

"Hungry, Wordsworth?" he said.

I immediately got up on my hind legs. Oooh, did my back hurt! I hadn't done that in years!

"Here you go." Mike tossed me a thick, juicy piece of roast beef. "Don't go anywhere. I want Alan to meet you."

He left. I chewed on the delicious food. Then Dee Dee arrived.

"Wordsworth!" She pointed at the roast beef. "How'd you get that?"

"A friend," I said in a low voice.

"Here he is," I heard Mike say. Looking up, I saw a man with a short, neatly trimmed white beard and glasses.

"That's some basset hound," the man said.

I finished my roast beef and got up on my hind legs again.

"Good dog." The man with the white beard smiled and handed me another piece of roast beef. Then he turned to Dee Dee. "Are you his owner?"

"Yes," Dee Dee said.

"A truly magnificent specimen," the man said. "How much does he weigh?"

"About eighty-five pounds," Dee Dee said. "The vet says he should lose weight."

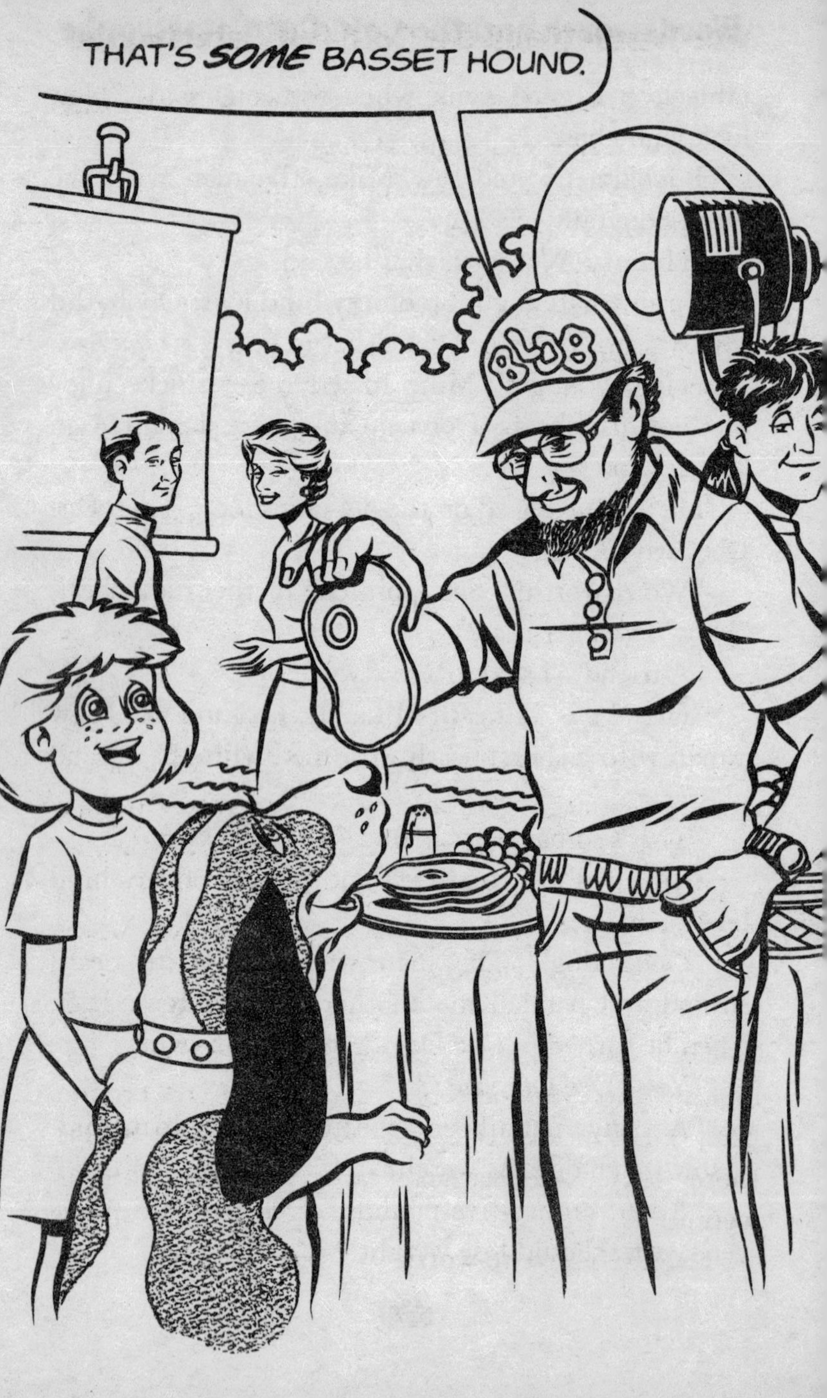
THAT'S *SOME* BASSET HOUND.

"Nonsense," the man said. "What do veterinarians know? I like a substantial dog."

That's what I was, a substantial dog.

"Are you Alan Roberts?" Dee Dee asked.

"Why, yes," the man said.

"I just love your movies," Dee Dee gushed. "I've seen *The Bride Wore Okra* and *Camp Slaughter.* My favorite's *The Thing from the Cuisinart.*"

"Thank you." Alan Roberts smiled. "That's one of my favorites, too."

"Do you think you could use Wordsworth in a movie?" Dee Dee asked.

"Oh, you never know," the film director said. "Right now I'm just worried about finishing *Chain-Saw Baby-Sitter* on time."

"What's the problem?" Dee Dee asked.

"The unions back in Hollywood," he said. "They move like molasses in January. I'm supposed to start shooting the interiors next week, but they're nowhere near being completed."

"Alan, we're ready to shoot the next scene," someone shouted from the set.

"Well, nice meeting you, Dee Dee," Alan Roberts said, shaking her hand. Then he gave me another piece of roast beef and patted me on the head. "And nice meeting *you,* Wordsworth. Don't let those silly veterinarians talk you into losing weight."

He didn't have to worry.

Dee Dee picked up my leash and led me home. She was unusually quiet.

"You're not mad that I ran away, are you?" I asked.

"No," she said. "I guess I was really hoping Mr. Roberts would want to use you in a film and we'd get a lot of money."

"Well, maybe someday," I said.

"Maybe, but that won't help us now," she said.

# Eighteen

**Bang! Bang! Bang! The next morning I** woke up to a terrible racket. It sounded like someone was hammering something in the front yard. I stretched and yawned, then went down the hall. I went out the front door to the porch. Leyland was standing in the front yard, banging into the ground a sign that said:

WELCOME TO THE CHANDLERS
A Bed & Breakfast
Vacancy

Flora stood a dozen yards away, making sure the sign was straight. Janine, Roy, and Dee Dee sat on the porch steps, watching. I lay down next to Dee Dee and she scratched me behind the ear.

"This is going to be a total disaster," Roy groaned.

"Great idea, Dee Dee," Janine said sarcastically.

"Maybe it'll work," Dee Dee said.

"Yeah, right." Roy rolled his eyes. "Did you see those old beds Dad dragged out of the attic last night? Half of them are ready to collapse. Dad was up past midnight taping them with duct tape."

"And those old mattresses." Janine pinched her nose closed with her fingers. "PU."

"It's all part of the charm," Dee Dee said.

"I'd rather be in a tent," Janine said.

Out on the front lawn, Leyland finished hammering the sign into the ground. "What do you think, darling?"

"It's a little bit crooked, but it will do," Flora said.

Mr. and Mrs. Chandler came back toward the porch.

"Well, children." Flora clasped her hands together. "Today marks a new chapter in our lives. We're embarking on an exciting new adventure in the world of hostelry."

"Who's going to clean the bathrooms?" Janine asked.

Leyland and Flora looked at each other.

"I haven't thought about that," Leyland said, rubbing his chin.

Flora turned to her oldest daughter. "Janine, darling . . ."

"Not a chance, Mom." Janine shook her head.

"Who's going to make them breakfast?" Roy asked.

"We're going to serve continental style, dear," Flora said. "Fresh breads and pastries from the bakery."

"And where are we going to get the money for that?" Janine asked.

"It won't take a lot," Leyland said. "We thought perhaps we could borrow some of your baby-sitting funds. . . ."

"I'm broke, Dad," Janine said.

Leyland looked at Roy, who shook his head. "Sorry, Dad, not a cent."

Next, he looked at Dee Dee, who also shook her head.

"Then we'll have to bake some bread of our own," Flora said. She marched past everyone into the kitchen.

"Mom, bake bread?" Janine shook her head wearily. "I can't wait to see this."

"Now, now, enough of this negativism," Leyland scolded her. "Your mother is a very talented cook when she puts her mind to it."

"Oh, Leyland?" Flora called from the kitchen.

"Yes, darling?"

"There are little brown things crawling around in the flour," she said. "Do you think that's all right?"

"I'll come take a look, darling," Leyland called back. Then he turned to the kids. "I'm going in to help your mother. If anyone comes to inquire about staying for the night, please try to be civil."

The kids bobbed their heads up and down. Leyland went into the house.

"What happens if someone dies while they're staying here?" Roy asked.

"I think it would be a problem," Janine said.

"Maybe we could just bury them in the backyard," Dee Dee said.

Janine glared at her. "Mom and Dad may be a little weird, but we're not the Addams family."

Dee Dee shrugged. "It was only a suggestion."

Janine went off to play tennis at the club. Roy went upstairs to watch TV and lift weights. Dee Dee went bike riding with her friend Kristen. I found a sunny spot on the porch and spent the day snoozing.

By dinnertime, no one had stopped to inquire about bed or breakfast. Everyone sat around the dinner table.

"Do you think we're doing something wrong?" Flora asked.

"No, darling," Leyland replied. "These things take time. No one knows that we're a bed-and-breakfast yet."

Janine leaned toward Roy and whispered, "If we're lucky, no one will find out."

Meanwhile, Flora glanced toward the kitchen counter, where three newly baked loaves of bread sat. "And I baked all that bread," she said with a sigh.

"What are those little brown specks, Mom?" Janine asked.

# Wordsworth and the Cold Cut Catastrophe

Flora shot Leyland a nervous look. "Oh, uh, protein, dear."

"A special recipe," Leyland added.

Just then there was a knock on the door. The Chandlers all looked at each other wide-eyed.

"Do you think?" Flora asked.

"Let's go see!" Dee Dee jumped out of her chair.

"Wait," Leyland said, rising. "I'll go. The rest of you stay here."

Dee Dee gave me a look. She wanted me to spy. I got up and went down the hall.

At the front door Leyland was speaking to a young couple. The man was wearing a white sweater and white pants. A pair of sunglasses hung from a string around his neck. The lady was also dressed in white. She wore lots of gold rings and bracelets.

"I saw your sign," the man said. "I'm Jim Porter and this is my wife Jessica."

"Delighted," Leyland said, shaking Mr. Porter's hand. "Would you like to come in?"

Mrs. Porter hesitated and pointed down at me. "Does he bite?"

"Only lamb chops," Leyland replied.

The Porters stepped in and looked around.

"Wow, what a funky place," Mr. Porter said.

"We've tried to preserve as much of the charm as possible," Leyland replied. "Would you like to see our rooms?"

"Sure," Mr. Porter said. But Mrs. Porter hesitated.

"What's with all the tape on the banister?" she asked.

"Oh, come on, babe," Mr. Porter said. "It just retro, that's all."

Leyland led the couple upstairs. I returned to the kitchen. Dee Dee gave me a questioning look, but of course I couldn't answer. A little while later Leyland came in with a smile on his face.

"Our first guests," he said, sitting down.

"They're staying?" Roy's eyes widened in amazement.

"Yes," Leyland said. "They've just gone for a walk in the park. Then they're going out for dinner. They'll be back around ten."

"You showed them their room?" Janine asked in wonder.

"Why, yes," Leyland said. "Mrs. Porter seemed a bit uncertain. But Mr. Porter was quite excited. He kept saying that it was all very retro. I'm not quite sure what he meant by that. Do you have any idea, darling?"

Flora shook her head.

"It means he thinks it's cool because everything is old and doesn't work," Janine said.

"Really?" Leyland's eyebrows rose. "In that case we're perfect for them."

# Nineteen

**What a night! I hardly got any sleep at all!** Mrs. Porter complained about everything! First it was about a toilet that wouldn't stop flushing. Then a light didn't work.

Upstairs, doors creaked open and closed. I heard mumbling and footsteps as the Porters moved from room to room, searching for one that fit their needs.

I managed to doze for a bit after that. Then the complaints started again. This time Mrs. Porter was unhappy about a torn window screen that let in too many bugs. More creaking of doors and footsteps followed, along with mumbling that often became grumbling.

Once again I slept, until a scream wrenched me from my dreams. Mrs. Porter was yelling something about mice. That was followed by the sounds of a loud, angry argument. Then Mrs. Porter came storming down the stairs, lugging a suitcase. She was followed by Mr. Porter and Leyland in his light blue pajamas and dark blue robe.

"But, honey, think of the stories we'll be able to tell our friends in the city," Mr. Porter said.

"I don't want stories," Mrs. Porter spit back. "I want to sleep without running toilets and bugs and mice."

"But that's what retro is all about, babe."

"You can have retro," Mrs. Porter snapped. "I'll take Holiday Inn."

She went out the front door and disappeared into the dark. Leyland, in his pajamas and robe, stopped by the door. Mr. Porter reached into his pocket and took out his wallet.

"Look, I'm awfully sorry," Leyland said.

"Hey, it's not your fault," Mr. Porter said. He took some bills out of the wallet and handed them to Leyland. "Jessica's just not into the retro experience. Frankly, I think you've really got a great concept here."

"Why, thank you."

Mr. Porter left. Leyland stared down at the bills in his hand. He shook his head in wonder, turned off the lights, and went back to sleep.

The next morning, everyone slept extra late. When they came into the kitchen, they all had puffy eyes.

"What time did the Porters leave?" Janine yawned and poured herself some cereal.

"Around four A.M.," Leyland said.

"It's too bad they missed out on Mom's protein bread," Roy said.

Without warning the kitchen lights went out.

"Now what?" Flora asked, looking around.

"We must've blown a fuse," Roy said, getting up. "I'll go look in the basement."

Janine frowned. "How could we blow a fuse? All we had on was a couple of lights."

A moment later Roy came back from the basement. "That's weird. All the fuses are okay."

"Maybe the whole area's lost power," Flora said.

"Uh, I don't think so," Roy said. He pointed out the window at the house across the street. "The Kreegers still have their outdoor lights on from last night. And the Pickneys' handyman is using an extension cord from their house to run the hedge trimmers."

"Then it's just our house," Dee Dee said.

"Yes, I'm afraid the electric company has terminated our service," Leyland said.

"What?" Janine gasped. Everyone stared at Leyland in disbelief.

"They've been sending threatening letters for months," Leyland explained. "We owe them a rather large sum of money."

"Why didn't you tell us?" Flora asked.

"I didn't want you to worry," Leyland said.

# Wordsworth and the Cold Cut Catastrophe

"Well, I'm going to call them right now and demand that they give us electricity," Flora said in a huff. She stood up and reached for the kitchen phone.

She started to dial, then stopped. "Oh, dear, the phone's dead."

"There must be one off the hook somewhere," Roy said, jumping up. "I'll go check."

"Don't," Leyland said.

Everyone stared at him again.

"Don't tell me they've disconnected the phones, too," Flora gasped.

Leyland nodded.

"Hooray!" Janine cheered.

"I thought it seemed awful quiet around here," said Roy.

"The phone company has also been sending me threatening letters," Leyland said.

"Oh, my." Flora looked very glum. "Things have gotten rather bleak, haven't they? We've got no money, no electricity, no phones, and hardly any food. Whatever shall we do?"

Dee Dee looked down at me with sad eyes. I knew what she was thinking. I could save the family by telling the world that I could talk. Of course it might mean that scientists would slice my brain into paper-thin pieces. But, on the other hand, the Chandlers would have their phone and electricity turned back on. They'd have food and probably enough money left over to fix the house up.

It would be a noble sacrifice.

Saving the Chandlers . . .

Future generations of basset hounds would be proud.

I'd prove once and for all that basset hounds are man's best friend.

I'd be a hero.

However, I preferred being a coward and keeping my brain intact.

Suddenly we heard loud knocking from the front door.

"Open up!" someone shouted. "This is the police!"

# Twenty

~~~~~~~~

**The Chandlers stared at each other**
wide-eyed.

"The police?" Janine frowned.

"Now what?" Flora asked.

"I suppose I'll have to go see," Leyland said reluctantly. Dee Dee gave me a look, so I went along.

Leyland answered the door. A short balding man wearing a gray suit was standing on the porch. Behind him was Mayor Pickney and a Village of Soundview police officer.

"Uh, Mr. Chandler?" the man in the suit said. "My name is Howard Blanco and I'm the attorney for the village."

"How may I help you?" Leyland asked.

"It has been brought to my attention that you are running a bed-and-breakfast establishment at this address," Mr. Blanco said. "Is that true?"

"Well, uh, er, yes, for the moment at least," Leyland replied. "I can't say it will continue much longer."

"But it's true that at this moment you are?"

"I suppose. Why?" Leyland asked.

"It is my duty to inform you that you have violated section seven, code five of town law, Mr. Chandler," the lawyer said. "The law states that you may not operate a commercial enterprise in a residential home. As a result you must be issued a summons to appear in court and pay a fine."

"A very substantial fine," Mayor Pickney added with a smile.

By now the rest of the family had joined us at the door.

"Isn't there anything we can do?" Roy asked.

"Yes, under section twelve, code nine, this property is zoned residential/commercial," Mr. Blanco said, taking a sheet of paper out of his briefcase. "If you would like, you can sign this affidavit declaring that you have commenced to operate a commercial enterprise from your home."

"That sounds reasonable," Leyland said.

"Wait a minute," said Janine. "There has to be a catch."

"There is, actually," said Mr. Blanco. "Once you sign this affidavit, you must come to town hall and purchase a commercial operations permit."

"A very expensive permit," Mayor Pickney added.

"And it also means that the taxes on your home will roughly triple," Mr. Blanco said.

Leyland handed the affidavit back to the lawyer. "We can't possibly afford that."

"Then you'll just have to pay the fine," Mayor Pickney said.

"But we can't afford to do that, either," Flora said.

"Well, that's life," Mayor Pickney said, turning to the lawyer. "What will happen if the Chandlers fail to pay their fine, Mr. Blanco?"

"Under section thirteen, code four," Mr. Blanco said, "the village would take possession of the property and sell it at auction. The proceeds of the sale would go toward satisfying the fine and whatever administrative expenses have been incurred. The remaining amount would then be turned over to Mr. Chandler."

"Very substantial administrative expenses, aren't they?" Mayor Pickney asked.

"Uh, yes, they tend to be," the lawyer said.

"So, Leyland, which would you like to choose?" the mayor asked. "The fine or the affidavit?"

"I just told you," Leyland said. "I can't afford either."

"I'm afraid you have to pick one or the other," Mr. Blanco said.

"I . . . I can't," Leyland said.

"Mayor Pickney," Flora said, "we've been your neighbors for fifteen years. We've never done anything to hurt you. Can't you do something to help us out of this?"

Mayor Pickney scratched his ear for a moment. "Well, there is one thing, but I'll have to speak to Leyland in private."

"All right," Leyland said. He followed the mayor down the porch steps and out onto the front walk.

I felt a foot nudge me. Looking up, I saw Dee Dee gesture that I should follow them. I went down the steps and stood beside Leyland while he and Mayor Pickney spoke quietly.

"Well, Chandler, looks like you're really stuck between a rock and a hard place now," the mayor said.

"Thanks to you," Leyland replied.

"Now, don't blame me," Mayor Pickney said. "I've been telling you for years to fix up your house. If you'd listened, this property would be worth three times as much as it is."

"Not everything in life has to be measured in dollars and cents," Leyland muttered.

"Maybe not." Mayor Pickney chuckled. "But you never had any sense, Chandler, and now you've got no cents either!"

Boy, did I want to take a bite out of him!

"Anyway, here's the deal," Mayor Pickney said. "I've got a friend, a real-estate agent, who'll buy this place from you right now for—" Mayor Pickney stretched up on his toes and whispered something into Leyland's ear.

# Wordsworth and the Cold Cut Catastrophe

Leyland frowned. "Surely my house is worth more than *that.*"

"Maybe, but you'll never find out, will you?" Mayor Pickney said. "Because if you don't take my friend's offer, the town will sell this house at auction. And believe me, you'll be lucky if you get *anything* after those administrative fees are taken out."

Leyland stared at Mayor Pickney and then started to walk away.

"Where are you going?" Mayor Pickney asked.

"Back to look at that affidavit for turning this into a commercial property," Leyland said.

"You're a fool, Chandler," Mayor Pickney hissed. "You'll never make this dump into a bed-and-breakfast. You'll never be able to afford the taxes. You don't even have the money for the permit!"

Leyland turned and stared at him. "I may be a fool, Mayor, but I'd rather see my money going to the village than to some friend of yours."

Bravo! I thought.

# Twenty-one

**The mayor and the lawyer left. The** Chandlers went back into the kitchen and sat down around the kitchen table. Leyland stared down at the affidavit.

"Dad, this is impossible," Janine said. "How are we going to turn this house into a successful bed-and-breakfast? The only guests we've had left in the middle of the night. And if they hadn't, Mom would've fed them homemade bread with little cooked bugs in it."

"And what about the commercial taxes and permit?" Roy asked. "How're we gonna afford that?"

"I spoke to Mr. Blanco," Leyland said. "The first tax payment isn't due for two months."

"But what about the cost of the commercial permit?" Flora asked.

"And what about paying the phone company and the electric company?" Roy asked. "People can't stay here if we don't have electricity."

"And what about the cost of fixing this place up?" Janine asked. "Fixing screens and faucets and beds and lights and getting rid of the mice?"

Leyland took a deep breath and let it out slowly. "My cousin Ned in New York is an antiques dealer. We have certain things in this house that he can sell for us."

"Not the family heirlooms!" Flora gasped.

"Yes." Leyland nodded sadly. "The gold mantel clock and the brass fireplace irons. The gold-leaf mirror and the sterling-silver flatware."

"But they've been in our families for generations," Flora gasped. "My parents would turn over in their graves if they knew we were selling them."

"Mine, too," Leyland said sadly. "But it's either the heirlooms or the house. And without the house we'd have no place to put the heirlooms anyway."

It was heartbreaking. I'd never seen the Chandlers look so sad. It was almost enough to make me consider trying dog food.

"Look," Roy said. "If that's what we have to do, I'm gonna sell my baseball cards to that store in town."

"I know a store that will buy my stuffed bears," said Janine.

"They'll probably take the rest of my dolls, too," said Dee Dee with a sniff.

"I suppose it's time to part with Aunt Matilda's lamp," Flora said sadly.

\*     \*     \*

The Chandlers spent the rest of the day collecting the family heirlooms. Then they packed them into boxes and put them in the car. Dee Dee sat on the porch steps and watched. I put my head in her lap. She scratched me behind the ear and looked very sad.

As evening fell Mayor Pickney looked over the fence at us.

"So, you're really going to try and get up the money for the commercial permit, huh?" he said.

"That's right," Leyland said.

"You know, Chandler, maybe you'll get lucky," Mayor Pickney said. "Maybe you'll get some suckers to stay in this dump of yours and you'll have enough to pay your taxes in two months. But that's because it's the summer now and everyone wants to be here. But what'll you do *after* the summer, huh? What'll you do in the winter when no one comes around? Forget it, Chandler. You'll never make enough to get through to next summer."

Roy looked up at his father. "Is he right, Dad?"

"I don't know, Roy," Leyland said. "Maybe."

"Then it really is hopeless," Roy said with sagging shoulders.

Dee Dee glanced down at me, and once again I knew what she was thinking. I was the one member of the family who could save them, the one member who had real earning power. If I didn't do anything, the Chandlers might lose their home in a few months.

And then they'd really be left with nothing.

It was a truly heartbreaking situation.

I felt tears drop onto my fur. I looked up and saw that they'd fallen out of Dee Dee's eyes.

"Please, Wordsworth?" she whispered. "You know how much I love you. I promise I won't let any scientists slice up your brain. You're the only one who can save us now."

All I had to do was say the word, *any* word, and I could save them.

I opened my mouth and . . .

Suddenly the scent of pastrami wafted my way.

I took off like a shot. I'd worry about saving the Chandlers later. Right now it was time to eat.

# Twenty-two

**Over on Elm Street they were just** putting away the cold cuts.

"Hey, look who's here!" Mike said, and tossed me a slice of pastrami. "It's Wordsworth. Hey, Alan, your friend's back."

Alan Roberts, the director, came over and scratched me behind the ear. "Hello there, Wordsworth. Come for some dinner, huh?"

I chewed happily on the pastrami.

"Looks like he came alone," Mike said. "Maybe I better take him home."

"Give him a moment to enjoy himself," Alan Roberts said. "We've got a big problem I need to discuss with you anyway."

"The interiors?" Mike guessed.

"Hollywood says they're two weeks behind," the director said. "If I have to delay shooting and keep everyone on payroll we'll go way over budget."

"What can we do?" Mike asked.

"Grooof!" I barked to get their attention.

"Oh, here you go, Wordsworth," Alan Roberts said. He took a piece of roast beef from the platter and tossed it to me. Then he turned back to Mike. "We've got all the film equipment here. We've got all the actors and actresses. I say we try to scout interiors here."

"You mean, shoot the scenes in someone's house?" Mike asked.

"Yes."

"But, Alan, you know how people hate that," Mike said. "We'd have to move into their house for a month! We'd have to completely redo the inside. Then it's day after day with dozens of people coming and going, electrical cables all over the place, a total mess, no privacy at all for anyone who lives there. No one in this neighborhood could be *that* desperate, no matter what you want to pay."

"We have to find a house," Alan Roberts insisted. "Find us a place to stay around here tonight. We'll start looking first thing in the morning."

My ears perked up. Did Alan Roberts just say he needed a place to stay? I knew just the place!

"Grooof!" I barked, and wagged my tail.

"Yes, yes, Wordsworth, I know you're hungry." Alan Roberts threw me another piece of roast beef. But for once I didn't want it.

"Look, he's shaking his head," Mike said.

"That's strange," said Alan Roberts.

Boy, if ever I felt like talking, it was right now! But I knew I couldn't. I had to do something really dumb and doglike. So I bit into the cuff of Alan Roberts's pants and started to tug.

"Hey!" Mike shouted protectively. "Let go of him, Wordsworth!"

"No, wait, wait," Alan Roberts said. "He wants me to go somewhere."

Smart man. I instantly let go and barked excitedly.

"We've finished shooting for the day," Alan said. "Let's see what he wants."

I led them back to the Chandlers' house as fast as I could.

Mike and Alan were both huffing and puffing by the time we got there.

"What in the world?" Alan Roberts stopped on the Chandlers' front lawn and stared up at the dilapidated house. The Chandlers were all out in front, loading the family heirlooms into the car.

"It's Alan Roberts!" Dee Dee gasped.

"Who?" asked Leyland.

"The one who does all those horror movies?" Roy asked.

While the kids rushed toward the famous film director, I went up to the bed-and-breakfast sign and pushed my paw against it.

"Hey, look at this," Mike said, waving Alan Roberts over. "Wordsworth must have heard us talking about a place to spend the night."

"You're right," Alan said, and looked down at me. "Smart dog."

Little did he know . . .

Mike looked back up at the house. "I don't know, Alan. It looks a little run-down."

"Oh, please stay," Dee Dee begged. "We really need the money. I promise we'll fix the screen and the toilet and the lights. And we'll try to get rid of the mice."

"Great sales job, Dee Dee," Janine said with a smirk.

"Actually, the great attraction of our place is the location," Leyland said. "As you can see, we're right across the street from Soundview Manor Park and Bell Island Sound."

"It's a lovely setting," said Flora.

"I'm sure it is," Mike said. "But we're not really here to sightsee."

"Oh." Both Leyland and Flora looked crushed.

"Please!" Dee Dee begged. "Please just have a look inside."

Alan Roberts and Mike gave each other a doubtful glance.

"All right," the director said. "A fast one."

Dee Dee ran up the broken front steps and pulled open the front door. Alan and Mike went up behind her and the rest of us followed.

When I got inside, Alan Roberts was standing in the front hall looking around with his mouth hanging open.

"My Lord," he gasped, as if stunned.

"Come on, Alan, let's go," Mike said. "This place is a wreck."

"Oh, no, please!" Dee Dee cried. "At least look at the bedrooms upstairs. Mom and Dad really fixed them up."

Dee Dee grabbed the director's hand and led him up the stairs. The rest of us stayed downstairs in an uncomfortable silence.

"Ahem." Mike cleared his throat. "Is it my imagination, or is that whole banister held together with duct tape?"

"It is." Janine nodded sadly.

"And how come it's so dark in here?" Mike asked. "Why don't you turn on some lights?"

"We, er, thought it added a sort of retro charm," Leyland ad-libbed.

"Retro, huh?" Mike rolled his eyes.

A few moments later we heard the stairs creak as Alan Roberts and Dee Dee came back down. The director still had a shocked look on his face.

"So, uh, what'd you think?" Roy asked hopefully.

"It's unbelievable," Alan said. "Absolutely horrible."

"I guess that means you won't be staying here tonight," Janine said.

Alan Roberts simply stared at her and didn't answer. Mike held open the door. "Uh, thanks everyone. I wish you a lot of luck with, uh, this place. Come on, Alan, we better get back."

They left.

Dee Dee sat down on the stairs and started to cry. I sat down next to her and put my head in her lap. I wished I could do something to make her feel better. But things really looked hopeless.

# Twenty-three

**That night, after it grew dark, the** Chandlers had no choice but to go upstairs to bed. A little while later I heard footsteps come down the stairs. Dee Dee came into the kitchen.

"Wordsworth?" she whispered.

"Yes?" I whispered back.

"We have to talk," she said.

"Hmmm." I had a feeling I knew what she was going to say.

"You're our only hope," she said, stroking my head softly. "You're the only one in the family who can make enough money to get us out of this mess. If you don't, we'll lose everything."

"I know."

"I realize it's a hard decision," Dee Dee said. "No one wants to have their brain cut into little pieces. But I promise I'll try not to let them."

"No offense or anything, Dee Dee," I said. "But

you're ten years old. I don't think you could stop them."

Dee Dee looked like she was going to cry. "Please, for the sake of our family, think it over."

"I will," I said.

Dee Dee leaned over and put her arms around my neck. She kissed me on the head. "I know you'll make the right decision."

I had a hard time sleeping that night. I tossed and turned. I dreamed the Chandlers were living in cardboard boxes under a highway somewhere.

In the morning, the Chandlers once again came down for breakfast with puffy eyes. It was obvious they hadn't slept much either. Dee Dee glanced at me and then turned to the others.

"Mom, Dad, everyone?" Dee Dee said. "Wordsworth has something he wants to tell you."

"Wordsworth?" Flora scowled at her.

"Hon, this isn't a good time for a joke," Leyland said.

"It's not a joke," Dee Dee said, turning to me. "Tell them, Wordsworth."

I started to open my mouth. Suddenly there was a knock on the door.

"Oh, dear, now what?" Flora sighed.

"Don't answer it, Dad," Roy said. "It's just going to be more bad news."

But the knocking continued and Leyland rose. "I'm sorry, everyone," he said. "I know I shouldn't answer it. But it's against my nature to be impolite."

"I'm going with you," Janine said, getting up. "I'm tired of all these people picking on you."

"Me, too," said Roy.

The next thing I knew, everyone marched down the hall to the front door. Janine pulled it open. A man in a blue suit stood outside, holding a briefcase.

"Forget it," Janine said. "We can't pay you. We don't have any money."

"That's not why I'm here," the man said.

"You can't have the house," said Roy. "Because we're gonna try to raise the money for the commercial permit."

"That's not why I'm here either," said the man.

"Why are you here?" Dee Dee asked.

"Please let me introduce myself," the man said. "My name is James Dunwright, and I'm a lawyer for Blob Productions."

He opened his briefcase and took out a thick sheaf of papers. He turned to Leyland. "Are you Mr. Chandler?"

"Yes," Leyland said.

"Then these are for you." Mr. Dunwright handed him the papers.

"Great," Roy groaned. "Now we're being sued."

"On the contrary," Mr. Dunwright said. "Blob Productions is Alan Roberts's film company. He is requesting the right to use your home and property for the interior scenes of *Chain-Saw Baby-Sitter.*"

The Chandlers all looked at each other in amazement.

"You want to use *our* house for the film?" Janine asked.

"Yes," Mr. Dunwright said. "Mr. Roberts feels that your home is perfect for a horror movie."

"I always knew it was perfect for *something,*" Janine said. "I just didn't know what."

"Now you've probably heard terrible stories about what film companies have done to houses before," Mr. Dunwright went on. "But this contract absolutely guarantees you that Blob Productions will leave your house with everything working. In fact, they promise to leave it in better shape than before they started."

"That won't be hard," Roy muttered.

"Uh, excuse me, Mr. Dunwright," Leyland said, pointing down at the contract. "But I think your typist made an error."

"Really? Where?" Mr. Dunwright slipped on his glasses and stared down at the contract.

"Uh, right here where it says payment," Leyland said. "Clearly there are too many zeros next to this number and the decimal is in the wrong place."

"No, sir." Mr. Dunwright shook his head. "This is the correct amount."

Leyland's eyes widened. "You're going to pay us *that* much to use our house for one month?"

"Yes, sir," Mr. Dunwright said. "And if we have to stay longer then one month, we will pay you a per diem of roughly twice the daily rate. Also, should it become necessary for your family to move out for part of the time, we will put you up in the finest hotel money can buy."

Leyland was speechless.

"There's just one thing," Mr. Dunwright said. "Mr. Roberts wants to start immediately. That means we'll have to apply for a commercial use permit right away."

"Why, I filled out the application last night," Leyland said, taking it off the mantel and handing it to him.

"Excellent," Mr. Dunwright said. "Then you have nothing to worry about. I'll take care of the permit. All you have to do is sign the contract."

Leyland signed the contract and handed it back to the lawyer.

"Great." Mr. Dunwright reached into his pocket and took out a light blue check. "This is a check drawn on the Bank of Hollywood for the first payment. The rest will come in weekly installments."

Mr. Dunwright offered his hand and Leyland shook it. "Thank you very much, Mr. Chandler. I assure you that you won't be disappointed with the improvements we'll make on your house. The only thing I'd advise you to do is remove everything that's fragile or of particular value. We just want to make sure we don't break anything."

"W-We . . ." Leyland stammered. "We've already done that. We packed all the family heirlooms and put them in the car."

"Well, then, you certainly are prepared. Good day, Mr. Chandler." Mr. Dunwright nodded and left. Dee Dee closed the door behind him.

"How much was the check for, Dad?" Roy asked.

"Look." Leyland held the check for everyone to see.

"Oh, wow!" Roy gasped. "That's enough to pay our taxes for years!"

"And it's only the first installment!" Janine gasped.

"This is a miracle!" cried Flora.

"And do you know who made it happen?" Leyland said. "Dee Dee."

"That's right," Flora said. "Dee Dee's the one who made Alan Roberts come in and look around."

"But Wordsworth was the one who got them to come over in the first place," Dee Dee said.

Everyone stared down at me.

"Wait a minute," Roy said. "Didn't you say before that Wordsworth had something to tell us?"

Dee Dee's eyes widened and she glanced nervously at me.

"Yeah, Dee Dee," Janine said. "What was Wordsworth going to say?"

"Uh . . . er . . ." Dee Dee stammered and looked at me for help.

# Wordsworth and the Cold Cut Catastrophe

"Grooof!" I barked.

Janine shook her head. "You are totally weird, Dee Dee."

# Twenty-four

⚮⚮⚮

**Leyland and Flora went to the bank** to deposit the check. Janine went off to play field hockey and Roy went back in the house to lift weights and grow muscles. Dee Dee sat on the porch. I lay on my back so she could scratch me under my chin.

"You must have heard them talking about needing a place to shoot the interiors, right?" Dee Dee asked proudly.

"Yup." I nodded. Why not take the credit?

"I'm really proud of you," Dee Dee said. "And just think, with the film crew here for a month, you'll have all the cold cuts you want."

Paradise, I thought with a smile.

"But you know what I'm most proud of?" Dee Dee asked.

"What?"

"This morning you were going to tell them you

could talk," she said. "You'd started to open your mouth."

"Yes," I said.

Dee Dee put her arms around my neck. "You were going to risk having your brain cut into little slivers just for the sake of our family."

Dee Dee hugged me and kissed my head. I nestled happily in her arms. The truth was, the only reason I'd opened my mouth that morning was to yawn. But, hey, Dee Dee didn't have to know that, did she?

**Todd Strasser** has written many award-winning novels for young and teenage readers. He speaks frequently at schools about the craft of writing and conducts writing workshops for young people. He lives with his wife, children, and dog in a place near the water.